"I have no intention of sleeping with you."

Roarke had the audacity to smile at her statement. A roguish grin that slashed white in his dark face and made his eyes gleam like sapphires. "Well, if you insist on splitting hairs, I think this is where I admit that *sleeping* wasn't exactly what I had in mind."

Sexual awareness hummed through her veins at his look, but Daria willed her voice to chipped ice. "Fine. Then let me be a bit more specific so you can understand. I'm *not* going to have sex with you."

Her voice might be cold, but Roarke could see something else in her eyes. Her words were what he'd been telling himself all morning while he'd been rattling around the kitchen, thinking of her lying upstairs in bed, all warm and soft. It was safer that way. Unfortunately, as he took in the sight of her wet and nearly naked body wrapped in a towel, he was struck with a sudden urge to lick those beads of moisture off the crest of her ivory breasts. Roarke had never been a really big fan of *safe*.

The author of over fifty novels, **JoAnn Ross** wrote her first story—a romance about two star-crossed mallard ducks—when she was just seven years old. She sold her first romance novel in 1982 and now has over eight million copies of her books in print. Her novels have been published in twenty-seven countries, including Japan, Hungary, Czech Republic and Turkey. JoAnn married her high school sweetheart—twice—and makes her home near Phoenix, Arizona.

Books by JoAnn Ross

HARLEQUIN TEMPTATION

Don't miss any of our special offers. Write to us at the following address for information on our newest releases.

Harlequin Reader Service
U.S.: 3010 Walden Ave., P.O. Box 1325, Buffalo, NY 14269
Canadian: P.O. Box 609, Fort Erie, Ont. L2A 5X3

ROARKE:
THE ADVENTURER
JoANN ROSS

Harlequin Books

TORONTO • NEW YORK • LONDON
AMSTERDAM • PARIS • SYDNEY • HAMBURG
STOCKHOLM • ATHENS • TOKYO • MILAN
MADRID • WARSAW • BUDAPEST • AUCKLAND

ISBN 0-373-25738-4

ROARKE: THE ADVENTURER

_____Prologue_____

Moscow

THERE WERE FEW pleasures as satisfying as spending a lazy rainy Sunday morning in bed with a gorgeous woman. Unfortunately, it seemed Roarke O'Malley was going to be deprived of such sensual delights this morning.

"I don't get it," he complained, hitching himself up in bed and putting one of the down-filled pillows behind his head. "You never work on Sunday. Hell, you never go to the studio before noon."

And she must be tired. They had spent most of the night at the Casino Royale, Moscow's most elegant casino, located in a palace once used by the czars whenever they came to the city for the horse races. Unlike the dark times under communist rule, these days Moscow's night life rivaled that of New York or Paris; the nightclubs didn't really start rocking until after midnight and didn't stop until sunrise. It had been only three hours since they'd returned to his hotel from the casino, and very little of that time had been spent sleeping.

"I told you, Anna called in with the flu," Natasha Adropov called out from the adjoining bathroom.

"Hell, she's probably just spending the day in bed with one of the station's cameramen." He scowled as

Natasha came out of the bathroom, enticingly clad in French lace underwear and smelling of the perfumed soap that was part of the five-star treatment at the Hotel Baltschug Kempinski Moskau. "Some women understand priorities."

She flashed him the smile that charmed Muscovites each evening on the national news. "Some women are content to stay weekend anchors."

Being ambitious himself, Roarke couldn't complain that Natasha was, without a doubt, the most driven woman he'd ever met. It was, after all, one of the things that had attracted him to her in the first place.

"Why don't you come back after the newscast?" he suggested. "We'll spend the afternoon driving each other crazy."

"That sounds lovely." She took a silk blouse and her new Armani suit from the closet. "But I'm afraid I've made other plans."

"Oh?" He narrowed his eyes. There was something new in her tone. He suspected she was hiding something. "I suppose, if you were spending the day with your old boyfriend, you'd let me know. Considering we're supposed to be collaborating on the story later, and all."

Natasha's former lover was a reputed kingpin in the Russian mafia. Apparently they'd grown up together in the same small town outside Minsk, and although she didn't seem to feel an intimate relationship between a news anchor and a mobster constituted a conflict of interests, whenever Roarke thought about it— which was increasingly often, given his own interest in the mafia wars currently taking place—he was decidedly uncomfortable with her slippery sense of morality.

Then again, he reminded himself, Russia wasn't America. The Puritans had never set foot in this country—and would undoubtedly be run out of Moscow if they showed up today—and given all she'd overcome in her life, he had no business judging her behavior. Especially since his relationship with Russia's sexiest newslady was simply business. With some hot, uncommitted sex on the side.

"Of course I'd tell you if I were meeting with Dimitri."

He wasn't sure he believed her. And experience had taught Roarke not to trust her. Even so, as she sat down in a brocade-covered wing chair and pulled on her stockings, he felt an automatic tug of desire.

"It's really too bad they have you behind a desk," he said, changing the subject. "Put you on a stool so viewers could get a look at those legs and your ratings would go through the roof."

She laughed at that. "My rating points are high enough to receive an offer from CNN, thank you."

"Really?" That was news to him. "When did that happen?"

"After I broke my story about the CIA operatives working on the *Moscow Times* editorial staff."

This was not Roarke's favorite subject. He folded his arms across his bare chest. "As I recall, that was originally my story."

This time her smile was professionally smooth and failed to reach her eyes. Dark eyes that had gone suddenly hard. "You weren't using it," she said reasonably.

"I was out confirming my sources."

She sighed, stood with a smooth, lithe movement and approached the bed on a feline glide that had attracted the attention of more than one male in the casino last night.

"Please, darling—" she ran her long, manicured fingers through his dark hair "—let's not rehash this old argument. After all, I've already apologized for the little misunderstanding." Her lips brushed lightly against his.

Misunderstanding, hell. She'd stolen his story right out from under him; a mere six hours after he'd foolishly shared it with her, she'd broken it on the air. By the next morning her broadcast had been picked up by networks around the globe, including his own.

Reminding himself that it was his own fault for not keeping his work closer to the chest, Roarke tamped down his renewed irritation and dived into the kiss, pulling her onto the bed with him.

"Roarke!" She wiggled, trying to escape his tight hold. "You're going to wrinkle my blouse."

"So, take it off."

"You know I can't." Once again her expression—and her tone—didn't match the look in her slanted brown eyes. Looking up at her, Roarke thought he detected an anxiety that went beyond a wrinkled silk blouse.

"Is everything okay?"

"Of course. It's just that if I don't leave now, I'm going to be late." She sat up and pressed her hand against his chest. "Perhaps I'll postpone my afternoon appointment. If I get back in time, we can go out to the champagne brunch at the Aerostar Hotel."

The hotel's wildly popular brunch was additional proof that Russia was not what it used to be. She could have been suggesting a typical Sunday at the Court of the Two Sisters back in Roarke's hometown of New Orleans.

"I'd rather just order room service. And eat it in bed."

"Whatever you want, darling." She kissed him again—a long kiss with promises of more to come—then stood and put on her coat.

"How do I look?"

He studied her, from the top of her sleek blond hair, down her lush ankle-length sable, to her buttery smooth Italian-leather pumps. "Like an advertisement for the glories of capitalism."

"Good. Because I want to impress ABC with today's broadcast."

"They made you an offer, too?" *When you're hot, you're hot*, Roarke thought.

"Don't tell a soul, but they're looking for a new backup for Ted Koppel."

"They offered you 'Nightline'?"

This time her smile reached her eyes, reminding him of a cat who'd just caught sight of a succulent bowl of cream. "Not yet," she admitted as she scooped up her suede Chanel handbag. "But confidential sources tell me that I'm at the top of a very short list."

She blew him a kiss and left the hotel room. Deciding to think about her riding to the American networks on his story later, Roarke closed his eyes and immediately fell asleep.

Less than five minutes later, she was back. "My car won't start. And the concierge told me there's a twenty-minute wait for a taxi."

Roarke found that news mildly amusing. At least

some things about Moscow hadn't changed. "Take my car. The keys are on the dresser."

"Are you certain? What if you want to go out?"

"I'm not going anywhere. I'm going to stay right here in bed and get some sleep to build up my strength for when you get back." He'd also decided that lifting some weights in the fitness center and swimming a few laps in the indoor pool would work out the hangover threatening behind his eyes.

"If you're sure—"

"Natasha, sweetheart, I'm sure. Take the damn car. After I get some sleep I'll call a mechanic to come look at yours."

"You are such a good man."

Her naturally husky voice wavered. And, amazingly, Roarke thought he viewed a glimmer of moisture in her eyes, then decided it must be a trick of the light. Natasha was, without a doubt, one of the toughest women—hell, *the* toughest person—he'd ever encountered.

He couldn't imagine her crying if someone ran over her pet dog. Not that she had one. That would entail some sort of personal commitment, and from what he'd seen, the lady was only committed to her career.

"That's me. Mr. Wonderful." He gave her another long masculine perusal and decided she was going to wow them at "Nightline." "Now, if you insist on working on a weekend, you'd better get going before I decide to drag you back to bed and show you just how good I can be."

She laughed at that. Only later would he realize that there was a hint of a choked-back sob in the sound, as well.

"*Prashchaytye,*" she said softly. Since her English

was as good as his—perhaps even better, since it lacked his Southern softening of consonants—he was momentarily surprised by her slipping back into her native Russian.

But before he could comment, she was gone again.

"*Prashchaytye,*" he murmured, finding it even odder that she'd chosen such a final farewell rather than *Do svidanya,* the Russian equivalent of "See you later."

"Aw, hell, what if she's going off to get herself involved in something dangerous?"

She was so damn cocky, it would be just like her to think she could pry more secrets out of the murderous crime boss without his suspecting anything. Clever, Natasha might admittedly be. But Dimitri Davidov hadn't gotten to the top of the former Soviet Union's organized-crime syndicate by being easily fooled. He was smart as a whip. He was also ruthless. And deadly.

Growing more uneasy, Roarke got out of bed and went over to the window. Through the rain-streaked glass he had a spectacular view of the heart of Moscow: the Muskva River, its banks dusted in a light winter-white coat of the season's first snow; the famed colorful onion domes of Saint Basil's Cathedral; Red Square, where a Christmas tree had actually been erected; and the crenelated walls and magnificent palaces of the Kremlin.

He saw her exit the hotel, viewed the doorman watching with undisguised admiration as she walked with that enticing, long-legged glide across Red Square to where he'd left his car this morning after discovering the gates to the parking garage were chained.

She looked up at the window, as if knowing she would find him standing there, and waved.

Deciding he was overreacting, Roarke waved back. "You've gotten so suspicious you probably wouldn't trust your own mother," he muttered to himself as he watched her put the key in the door lock.

The explosion rocked the nine-story hotel, rattling the window glass.

"No!" Roarke shouted as he stared at the blinding orange fireball where his Mercedes had been parked only seconds before.

1

Two months later

IT WAS MARDI GRAS in the Big Easy, the last gasp of high frivolity before the austerity of Lent. Since it seemed as if the entire city of New Orleans was taking part in the public party, a dead man was the last thing Daria Shea had expected to find in her hotel room.

At first, she didn't realize that he was, indeed, dead.

"You're late," she scolded the man slouched in the wing chair by the window overlooking the inner courtyard. She tossed her purse and the bag of *muffulettas* and drinks onto the table. "I figured we should work through dinner, so I got us some sandwiches."

Taking his silence for the disapproval she'd come to expect, she responded with the defensiveness he always provoked. "It's a madhouse out there. Even if we *were* fortunate enough to find a vacant table anywhere in town, we'd never have any privacy."

Still, nothing. He continued to stare at her, as mute as one of the hand-painted coconuts tossed to the crowds by riders on the Zulu krewe float. Surely he wasn't angry because she hadn't been sitting around waiting for him to arrive from Washington? After all, *he* was the one who was late. Frustrated, she took two bottles from the brown paper bag. Mineral water for her, a Dixie beer in a long-necked bottle for him.

"Didn't your mother ever tell you that sulking was unattractive?"

When she still received no response, Daria felt a stirring of unease. "Martin?" She moved toward him. "This isn't funny." Her blood chilled, her heart began to beat faster. "Dammit, Martin—"

She reached out to shake his shoulder, but the moment she touched him, U.S. Federal Attorney Martin Fletcher's lifeless body slumped forward and fell onto the pale green carpeting.

Covering her mouth to hold back her scream, Daria grabbed her purse and fled the room.

ROARKE DECIDED THAT the Blue Bayou Lounge, just off the lobby of New Orleans's Whitfield Palace Hotel, resembled the bar scene from *Star Wars*. A nearly seven-foot-tall Marie Antoinette—sporting a towering powdered wig and suspicious Adam's apple—was engaged in spirited conversation with a man dressed as an oversize condom and a voluptuous redhead whose black leather bra, matching short shorts, thigh-high boots and whip were enough to make any S&M devotee swoon.

A man clad in a silver-lamé body stocking, oversize feather-covered wings and a jeweled halo danced with a nun to an earsplitting rendition of "Long Tall Sally." At the edge of the postage-stamp-size dance floor, a trio of buffed-up musclemen made up to resemble the cop, the Indian, and the cowboy of Village People fame compared pecs and biceps.

"I just love Mardi Gras, don't you?" a female voice inquired.

Reminding himself that if he'd been searching for solitude, he never should have returned home to New Orleans during Mardi Gras, Roarke reluctantly turned toward the newcomer who'd latched on to the just-abandoned barstool beside him.

"Nothing like it," he agreed.

The blonde was wearing what appeared to be a dress of gold chain-mail. The only thing she had on beneath the see-through minidress was a silver G-string. When the sight of her wondrous, obviously surgically enhanced breasts stirred not a single responsive chord inside him, Roarke reluctantly wondered whether his network bureau chief might have had a point when he'd accused him of being dangerously burned-out.

He hadn't hurt Dimitri Davidov that badly, Roarke thought. A few broken bones, some cracked ribs. Okay, there had been that little matter of a knife wound that had punctured a lung, but he'd been acting in self-defense at the time, so that shouldn't even have been considered.

"Excuse me?" he asked when he realized the golden girl with the south-of-the-Mason-Dixon-line drawl was talking to him again.

"I asked if you were from New Orleans."

Before Roarke could answer that he wasn't really from anywhere, anymore, a brunette wearing a clinging black cat-suit and a jet mask covering the top half of her face suddenly rushed up to him, threw her arms around his neck and kissed him. Smack on the mouth.

Her lips were as soft as magnolia petals and as Roarke found himself surrounded by a light romantic scent, he felt a stir of desire. Not that unsurprised by her behavior—he'd certainly witnessed far more bizarre events during Mardi Gras—Roarke decided not to question the reason for her unexpected kiss.

After all, before what his superiors were referring to as "O'Malley's Major Screwup," he'd built an enviable career as a hotshot, newsbreaking war correspondent on his ability to go with the flow.

Enjoying the rise of hunger he'd thought had been blown to smithereens on a city street in Moscow, and curious to see just how far she was willing to take this, he put his hands on the appealing stranger's slender waist, intending to draw her closer, when she suddenly pulled away.

"Wherever have you been, darling? I promised Jan and Harvey that we'd meet them at Petunia's for dinner nearly a half hour ago. I am just dying for a big helping of shrimp Creole. And you know how I am about indulging my cravings."

Although the mask kept him from getting a good look at her face, through the slanted catlike holes that had been cut for her eyes, Roarke caught a glitter of an emotion that looked a lot like passion.

Taking hold of his hand, she practically dragged him off the oak barstool.

"I have no idea who Jan and Harvey are," Roarke drawled as she weaved her way through the crowd, "but that little bit about satisfying your cravings has definitely piqued my interest, sweetheart."

Her eyes, he noticed, were never still; they fluttered about the lounge like trapped sparrows seeking some way to escape.

"Please," she murmured, her fingers tightening on his as they crossed the crimson-and-gold carpeting of the hotel lobby, "just play along with me and don't ask any questions until we get out on the street."

A warning sounded in Roarke's mind, followed by a flashback of the explosion that had rocked downtown Moscow and left a hole the size of a city bus where his car had been parked.

She might look like Cat Woman, smell like his mother's garden and taste like honey, but Roarke had been down this dead-end road before.

"Look, sweetheart—"

"Please." Her voice vibrated with strain. Her entire body radiated a watchful stress that he could easily recognize, having experienced it more than a few times himself. "I promise, I just need you to help me escape the most obnoxious man."

Daria had recognized him the moment she'd run into the Blue Bayou. Roarke O'Malley was a familiar sight on network television, looking wonderfully dashing as he covered wars in all the far corners of the globe. So dashing, in fact, that tabloid stories about his rumored hedonistic love-life were always popping up on the rack in her supermarket.

Although she had no idea what he was doing here, in New Orleans, she *did* know that he represented safety. He was, after all, the only man in the city she was certain wasn't out to kill her.

But his in-depth reporting had also revealed that he was more than a ruggedly handsome network face. He was intelligent enough to spot a lie a mile away. She thought about telling him the truth, even asking for his help, but having dealt with the media enough to fear that he would break the story before she could arrange for protection, Daria couldn't risk trusting him.

Fortunately, although she'd always been a rotten liar, her trial experience had taught her to bluff.

Although she was desperate to escape, she paused long enough to give him a dazzling smile designed to bring the most hard-hearted male to his knees. "He was the quintessential blind date from hell." Her fingers began stroking his sleeve in a seemingly unconscious seductive gesture.

She was good, Roarke allowed. Damn good. But she was also a liar. Then again, he'd learned the hard way that women were not above telling whatever lies it took to get what they wanted from a man. Or, he reminded himself, to set a guy up for murder.

"Why me?"

"What?" Impatience, nervousness—perhaps even fear—surrounded her like an aura, arousing his curiosity.

"Why did you pick me to help you escape the date from hell?"

"Oh." She took a deep breath that drew his attention momentarily to her breasts, which, while not nearly as voluptuous as those of the lady in chain mail, filled out the cat-suit just fine. "You looked safe." Her masked gaze moved from the top of his dark head, down to his feet, then back up again. "And large."

"Large enough to handle most ill-behaved dates," he agreed, deciding to play along for now. "Unless the guy's a linebacker or pro wrestler."

"No." She frowned. How could she explain that she had no idea what her potential assassin looked like? "At least, I don't think so."

She shook her head as her frightened eyes skimmed the lobby the same way they had the cocktail lounge, lighting on each person as if looking for someone in particular. When a dark-suited man emerged from behind a marble pillar, headed their way, Roarke felt her stiffen.

"Could we continue this conversation some other time? You're drawing attention to us."

She began walking toward the bronze revolving door again. Since she had hold of him, Roarke went with her. He would have gone with her even if she hadn't had that death grip on his arm.

"If you're not interested in attention, you shouldn't run around dressed like that," he advised. "And how come you don't know what the guy does for a living?"

"It's Mardi Gras," she said, as if that explained the outfit and her behavior. Which, Roarke guessed, it pretty much did. "What guy?"

"Your date," he reminded her, deciding she wasn't as deft a liar as he'd first thought.

"Oh... Him... Well, we, uh, didn't get to discussing occupations."

"Sounds like dislike at first sight."

"I'm fairly good at reading people. At least most of the time," she muttered.

They were outside on the sidewalk, which was packed with people lined five deep, shoulder to shoulder, to watch the night's parade. Several were holding umbrellas turned inside out in hopes of snaring "throws" to take back home along with their hurricane glasses and gris-gris voodoo charms as souvenirs of the vacation of a lifetime. Throw catching was serious business; Roarke had witnessed benign-appearing, lavender-haired grandmotherly types stomp a man's knuckles bloody in a contest for a string of fake pearls or a plastic doubloon.

The sky was overcast with heavy clouds that had caused the temperature to drop at least twenty degrees since he'd arrived at the airport three hours earlier. The scent of threatening rain rode on the cooling air and the wind was beginning to pick up, rattling the wide green leaves of the banana trees in a neighboring courtyard.

"You realize, of course, that Petunia's is going to be packed tonight."

She looked up at him and shook her head. "Don't be silly. I have no intention of going to Petunia's. Not after announcing it to the entire Blue Bayou Lounge." When a mounted patrolman rode by, the horse's hoofs clip-clopping on the pavement, she quickly turned away.

"Look," Roarke said, getting tired of the game playing, "why don't we just cut the bullshit. If some guy's really giving you trouble, we can just stop that cop and—"

"No." Her answer was quick, her voice strained. Her eyes, illuminated by the flashing lights of the strip joint across the street, had that frightened-bird look again. "Really, there's no need for that." She rose up on her toes and kissed his cheek. "Thanks for the assistance. It's nice to know that Southern chivalry still exists."

He should have been prepared. Especially after that debacle in Moscow. But the momentary touch of her lips against his skin distracted him enough to allow her to suddenly break loose and meld into the teeming crowd of merrymakers.

"Damn!" He slammed his fist into his palm. Unaccustomed to failure, and sensing a story when he stumbled across one, Roarke took off after her.

DARIA'S HEART WAS pounding in her ears as she tried to make her way through the Mardi Gras crowds. She wondered why Martin's killer hadn't waited for her in the hotel room. Perhaps he'd thought it too risky. But she knew he would come after her, knew her assassin could be any of the masked and costumed throng—Pan, perhaps, or Ra, the gilded sun god who suddenly appeared in front of her, grabbed the tops of both arms, and stopped her scream by brazenly stealing a kiss. She felt the scrape of a tongue stud against the inside of her mouth before her amorous assailant moved on to the next available female.

A hand grabbed her bottom and squeezed. Not wanting to draw attention to herself by confronting whoever dared such familiarity, she pulled away, her head spinning, her vision fogged from panic as she continued on, with no firm destination in mind, only knowing that the farther away from the police station she got, the safer she would be.

She turned the corner at Saint Peter Street and headed away from the river, pushing her way through the laughing, boisterous crowd. Despite the noise surrounding her, the sound of her high heels, clattering on the pavement, reverberated in Daria's ears like gunfire.

Her nerves were horribly on edge, and a scream bubbled up in her throat as she was suddenly pulled into a circle of drunken men.

"What's the hurry, darlin'?" one of them asked as he pulled her up against him, rubbing his body lewdly against hers, while another man pressed in from behind.

Furious and terrified all at the same time, she jammed her high heel into his instep.

Cursing viciously, he released her long enough to

allow her to take off running again. She nearly knocked over a trio of elderly nuns who'd come out to observe the festivities and considered turning to them for help, but not wanting to get them involved in something so deadly, she continued on, not knowing where the killer might be. Or who he might be.

She reached Rampart Street, which under normal circumstances would be nearly deserted. However, during the eleven parade days of Mardi Gras, people jammed the street, waiting for the colorful line of floats that would pass by on their way to Municipal Auditorium in Louis Armstrong Park.

Several of the lights on the arch leading into the park had burned—or been shot—out and she knew that even with all the witnesses, to enter the park at night could be a fatal mistake. To follow Basin Street would be no safer. It cut a winding path between the park and Saint Louis Cemetery No. 1, a place that no cautious woman would venture into during the day, let alone at night.

Daria was attempting to figure out which way to go when she was suddenly grabbed from behind. A broad leather-gloved hand covered her mouth, trapping her breath. As she was pulled back against the man's side, she caught a glimpse of a black executioner's hood. With arms that felt like steel cables holding her against him, her attacker dragged her toward the cemetery.

"Hey, man!" a college student wearing a Tulane sweatshirt called out. "What do you think you're doing?"

"My wife and I had a little argument," the man said in a pleasant voice that was at direct odds with the way his fingers were digging into her flesh beneath the Lycra cat-suit. "I'm just taking her somewhere we can talk in private."

The kid looked unconvinced. "Are you all right, ma'am?"

Her captor was holding her so tightly against him she could feel the unmistakable shape of a gun in the pocket of his trench coat. "Say everything's fine," he hissed into her ear, his breath hot and smelling of bourbon, "or the kid's a corpse."

Since he was radiating evil intent, Daria believed him. "Everything's fine," she said as instructed, inwardly cringing as she heard the shaky fear in her voice.

The Tulane student gave her another look. Then, as his companions called out for him to hurry up, he shrugged, obviously deciding that his assistance wasn't needed.

"Good girl," the man grated. "Now, here's what we're going to do. You're going to come with me. I've got a friend of yours who wants to have a little heart-to-heart chat with you."

Daria knew there would be no chat. What she knew was too dangerous to allow her to live. They were going to kill her. Just like they'd killed poor Martin.

Adrenaline pumped through her veins, giving her the strength to break away. But the man leaped after her, caught her flowing hair and hurled her roughly to the ground. She struggled to her knees and looked up at the assassin. The eyes visible through the holes in the black hood resembled those of a tiger who'd just caught sight of its prey.

Daria struggled to swallow her fear and forced her mind to remain calm. She was an intelligent woman. Hadn't she graduated first in her class at Stanford law school? Hadn't she made law review? Hadn't she been on the short list to clerk for a state supreme court justice when she'd accepted the position in the prosecutor's office? Surely she could think of a way out of this predicament.

"You'll never get away with this," she warned as her heart drummed impossibly hard against her ribs.

"Want to bet?" His voice was deep and rough and filled with deadly intent. "You should have left well enough alone, bitch. Now you're going to find out what happens to a woman who puts her nose in other people's business."

He jerked her to her feet and began half dragging, half marching her into the darkened cemetery. The shells used for gravel in this part of the world crunched beneath their feet; the white marble tombs gleamed ghostlike in the silver winter moonlight that had managed to slip between a gap in the heavy black rain clouds.

"This is far enough." He flung her against one of the larger tombs. As she hit her head on the stone and slid to the ground, Daria found it ironic that of all the places he could have picked to kill her, he'd chosen Marie Laveau's final resting place. The X's drawn on the tomb had been made by individuals hoping that New Orleans's former voodoo queen would grant their wishes; the coins, shells and beads scattered at the base of the tomb had been left as payment.

He'd just knelt beside her and taken the pistol she'd felt earlier from his pocket when two African-American teenagers suddenly appeared from behind the tomb.

"Police," her captor growled.

It was all that needed to be said. They both looked

from Daria to the man, to the gun, then turned and began to run back toward the red-brick housing project. Although she suspected their reasons for being in the cemetery in the first place hadn't been exactly legal, Daria had no intention of risking their lives by calling out for help.

"Now then, where were we?" Daria found his pleasant tone every bit as terrifying as the gun barrel he'd just pressed against her temple. The gun, she noticed, was equipped with a silencer. This was a man comfortable with killing; he would suffer no pangs of conscience after pulling the trigger.

Unable to draw a breath to scream, but unwilling to die without a struggle, Daria surreptitiously gathered up a handful of shells.

"I don't understand what you're talking about," she managed, choking back her terror.

"You realize that if you die with a lie on your lips, you go to hell," he said conversationally. He'd become slightly winded from dragging her into the cemetery. Now that he'd caught his breath, he seemed to be enjoying his role of assassin.

"It's not a lie—"

He hit her—a hard, backhanded blow that jerked her head back—then surprised her by running his gloved fingers down her throbbing cheek in an evil parody of a caress. "It's a shame we don't have more time," he murmured. "You're an appealing package."

The hand trailed down her throat, his thumb lingering at the hollow where her blood was pounding wildly. "I've never been able to figure out what you saw in that jerk you got yourself engaged to. Always looked like a pansy to me. Too bad you're going to die without ever knowing how good it can be with a real man."

She swallowed back the bile that rose in her throat. An idea occurred to her. One that was every bit as dangerous as it was outrageous. "Why does it have to be that way?"

He lowered the zipper on the front of the cat-suit, revealing pale flesh that contrasted vividly with her jet lace bra.

"What way?" He trailed the barrel of the gun between her breasts, obviously enjoying her involuntary tremors.

"If you really are going to kill me—"

"Oh, I am."

"Well, now that you've brought the subject up, I don't think I want to die a virgin."

Bingo. She knew she'd just said the magic word when the gun stilled and his eyes jerked up to hers. "You're lying."

"There's one way to find out."

"You're engaged."

"So? I'm an old-fashioned girl. And besides," she improvised, "you're right about James. The one time we almost did it..." She paused for dramatic effect, trying her best to appear embarrassed rather than terrified. "Well, he couldn't quite, well...you know."

He threw back his head and laughed at that. The rough sound scraped against her nerve endings like sandpaper. "Figures."

"Even condemned prisoners get a last request," she reminded him.

He reached under the hood and rubbed his jaw as he seemed to be considering that. "If you're trying to pull something, I'll kill you."

"You're going to kill me anyway," she said. "I'm just trying to get something out of the experience."

He gave her a long deep look. "You lawyers always have to dicker."

"I think it's in our blood."

As he continued to look at her breasts, his laugh was softer. And far more deadly. "You know, I must be nuts. Because I'm actually considering going along with this."

"I wish you would." She took off her mask and tried for what she hoped was a seductive expression. "I'm asking you to make a woman of me. Then you can do anything you want. Kill me, if you insist. But there's always the chance we'll be so good together, you'll want to keep me. No one would ever need to know."

"Always liked the idea of a love slave," he mused out loud. "Read a story in *Rawhide*." Daria was not surprised when he named one of the most lewd porno magazines. The vice guys had brought some in after a recent kiddie-porn raid and although she'd never considered herself a prude, the acts of sadomasochism portrayed in the magazine's pages had quite literally turned her stomach.

"Guy was in a custody battle with his wife," he related, "so he took her lawyer captive. The bitch had to do everything he wanted her to do—*everything*," he stressed wickedly, "or he'd cut little pieces off her."

Daria couldn't help it. She shuddered. "You wouldn't have to cut me," she promised. "I'd do whatever you wanted. In fact—" reminding herself that desperate situations called for desperate measures, she reached up and pressed her palm against the swelling visible at the front of his jeans "—I want to."

When he stirred against her hand, Daria feared she would throw up. Reminding herself that the objective was to survive, she managed, just barely, to keep her revulsion to herself.

He glanced around the deserted cemetery. "Not here," he decided.

"Where?"

"In the bayou. That way no one can hear you scream."

Daria knew that if she allowed him to take her away from the city, out into that dark and dangerous place, she would never survive.

He jerked her to her feet with a force that caused a cracking sound in her shoulder joint and made her flinch. Then, as if wanting to stake his claim on her now, he pulled her against him, much as the drunken men in the street had done, ripped off the executioner's hood and ground his mouth against hers so hard their teeth clashed.

His hand was tangled in her hair, effectively holding her hostage. His thick tongue was down her throat in a way that almost made her gag. The punishing kiss was nothing like the surprisingly stimulating one she'd shared with Roarke O'Malley earlier.

That thought led instantly to another. If she hadn't run away from the reporter, she wouldn't be in this fix now.

But she had run away. And never having been one to dwell on what might have been, Daria knew her survival was strictly in her own hands.

Having no intention of going meekly to her death, she jammed her knee up between his legs. When he dropped to his knees, she threw the shell gravel with all her strength into his face.

His roar reverberated off the lonely tombs like that of a wounded lion. She wheeled away and began running toward the street—and, she prayed, safety.

Jo Leigh

2

IT DIDN'T TAKE LONG to find her. A mere ten minutes after she'd managed to slip away from him, Roarke was headed down Rampart Street when he came across a crowd gathered in a circle beneath the spreading yellow glow of a streetlight. At the center of the circle, a uniformed cop stood guard over an unconscious woman.

Although she was facedown, Roarke had no trouble recognizing the clinging black cat-suit. She was lying in a pool of darkening blood that was being washed away by the light winter rain that had begun to fall. A slender black shoulder bag was on the ground beside her.

Using his size to his advantage, he pushed his way through the crowd. "Roarke O'Malley," he said, flashing his press badge at the cop. "WorldWide Broadcasting Network. What happened?"

The policeman, who didn't look old enough to shave, seemed unimpressed by Roarke's credentials.

"When I say everybody stand back, I mean everybody. Including reporters." His scornful tone gave Roarke the distinct impression that the news media were ranked with drug dealers and serial killers on his personal hierarchy.

Roarke hadn't made it to the top of a very exclusive ladder without being able to think on his feet. He also had no intention of letting the woman lying on the pavement out of his sight again. "I'm more than a reporter," he retorted. "I just happen to be the lady's husband."

A murmur rippled through the crowd. The suspicious expression didn't leave the cop's face, but his shrug said he wasn't going to bother arguing the point.

"You and the little woman in town on vacation?"

"Yeah."

Roarke knelt down beside the prone woman. Her hair was wet with rain and a dark sticky substance that could only be blood. Someone—the cop?—had taken her mask off, revealing a face he knew under normal conditions would be lovely, but was at the moment far too pale.

"Funny you weren't together. Like most folks on vacation."

"We got separated in the crowds. That's easy to do this time of year." Roarke wondered if he'd suddenly become a suspect. That was all he needed. "We should be doing something for her, dammit." He shrugged out of his leather bomber jacket and laid it over her.

"I called in for an emergency vehicle," the cop said back defensively.

She'd been shot. Roarke had seen enough gunshot wounds to recognize the bullet graze on her scalp.

"Wife gets shot," the cop said, as if quoting the police manual, "first suspect is usually the husband."

"Yeah, I've watched 'Homicide,' too." Watching the anger move across the kid cop's face, Roarke reminded himself that sarcasm wasn't going to help keep him out of an interrogation room.

"Maybe it was an accident. Someone shooting a gun

off in the air," he suggested. "What goes up, comes down."

The cop frowned. "Too many damn civilians shooting guns during Mardi Gras."

"Isn't that the truth." It was not Roarke's nature to be polite and obliging, but he could be, when necessary. "It's a wonder half the city isn't lying bleeding in the street." He pushed her matted hair away from her temple. She was too pale; her complexion reminded him of the shells underfoot everywhere in the city. "Where the hell is that ambulance?"

Right on cue, a battered red-and-white ambulance came screaming up, scattering the crowd. The rotating red lights atop the ambulance were reflected in the puddles on the street, giving a surrealistic look to the somber scene.

"Where are you taking her?" he asked the paramedic taking her blood pressure and pulse while the other set up an IV.

"Tulane."

"Hey," the cop said suddenly, "did you say your name was O'Malley?"

"Yeah."

"You Mike O'Malley's hotshot reporter brother?"

"Mike's my brother." The hotshot remark didn't sound like a compliment, but Roarke wasn't going to rise to the bait. "You know him?"

The cop shrugged. "Everyone knows Mike. We were real sorry he quit the force after that serial-rapist thing."

Roarke didn't want to waste time discussing his big brother's disaffection with the New Orleans police force. "Can't blame a guy for wanting to be his own boss."

"No." The cop frowned, as if wondering what his superiors would want him to do now.

"Look, officer," Roarke said as the paramedics lifted the woman onto a gurney. "I know how understaffed the department is during carnival. Why don't I go to the hospital with my wife while you track down some detectives to send over to interview us?"

The young cop looked from Roarke to the unconscious woman, then back to Roarke again. "Well, I guess that'd be okay," he decided. "Seeing as she can't tell me anything right now and you're Mike's brother."

"If you're coming along, let's get going," the paramedic complained. "Unfortunately, the lady isn't the only customer we've got tonight."

Deciding not to give the cop the opportunity to change his mind, Roarke scooped up the purse and jumped into the back of the ambulance. As they slogged through the crowds clogging the streets, lights flashing and siren blaring with scant effect, Roarke reached out to take her hand in his.

The diamond solitaire glittering like ice on the third finger of her left hand was only one of the reasons he hadn't believed that little story about a blind date.

"Who are you?" he murmured as he absently stroked a finger down the back of her limp hand.

As if his words had managed to filter through whatever fog was clouding her mind, her eyes suddenly opened. They were the color of aged whiskey, laced with pain and, he thought, fear.

"Please." Her voice was too soft for the paramedics, who were currently arguing about the fastest route through the carnival crowd, to hear. "Don't let them kill me."

He leaned down, ostensibly to stroke her face. "Who would want to kill you?"

Her eyelids fluttered shut. She murmured something he couldn't quite make out.

His mouth was next to her ear. "I can't help you if you don't tell me who *they* are."

Her eyes didn't open. He could feel her drifting away again. Just when he thought he'd lost her completely, she managed to whisper, "Police."

His WBN bosses had told him that he was burnedout. Maybe even finished. And although he would never admit it to another living soul, deep down inside, when he'd boarded that plane under government police escort in Moscow forty-eight hours ago, Roarke had figured they were probably right.

But now that he'd gotten himself tangled up with Cat Woman, whoever she was, Roarke was discovering, to his chagrin, that old impulses died hard.

He picked up her purse from the floor of the ambulance and opened it. He bypassed a lipstick tube and birth-control-pill compact and pulled out her billfold. Her Louisiana driver's license listed the usual information—height, weight, eye and hair color. And her name—Daria Shea. Although her expression was serious, her photo was better than the usual bureaucratic photo, which wasn't surprising, given her looks.

The wallet also contained twenty dollars in cash, an AMEX card and a Visa. Nothing out of the ordinary.

"Bingo." He whistled beneath his breath as he got to an ID card identifying her as a deputy prosecutor. Which only made the mystery more intriguing. He had no idea if she was telling the truth, but if she was, he'd definitely stumbled onto something worth looking into. It wasn't every day cops were trying to kill someone who was supposedly on the same side.

BUSINESS WAS BRISK in the emergency department at Tulane University Medical Center. A steady stream of patients arrived by ambulance, taxi, private car and even on foot. The injured were mostly in costume, as were many of the medical staff treating them.

Impatient, frustrated and wondering why a simple CAT scan could be taking so long, Roarke cooled his heels in the waiting room.

As he watched a woman dressed like the Little Mermaid have a cut above her eye stitched up by a six-foot-five-inch African-American genie, he'd just about decided to go looking for his mystery woman when Michael Patrick O'Malley arrived at the hospital.

"Nice of you to let the family know you were coming home," he greeted his brother dryly.

"I didn't have a lot of advance warning."

Mike pulled back from the fraternal hug and gave his younger brother a long look that Roarke figured probably had worked wonders during interrogations. "Sounds like those rumors that popped up on CNN last week might have some basis in fact."

Roarke wasn't in the mood for the third degree. He'd spent the flight back to the States stuck next to a Russian weight-lifter who seemed to be auditioning for a job as a stand- up comedian.

As soon as he'd landed at Kennedy, he'd been whisked by limousine to the network offices where he'd been forced to undergo a furious dressing-down by Darren Fairfield, president of WorldWide Broadcasting Network, that had resulted in Roarke's tossing his press badge on the wide mahogany desk.

Fortunately, Jordan Conway, VP and head of the news department, had leaped into the breach, soothing tempers and suggesting a cooling-off period for all parties concerned.

Roarke had reluctantly agreed to a temporary leave of absence, had booked himself a seat on the next available flight to New Orleans, where, after checking into the Whitfield Palace, he'd wandered into the lounge for a drink and met Cat Woman. Although this wasn't the first time he'd been awake for forty-eight hours straight, fatigue was beginning to catch up with him.

"I didn't kill anyone," he grumbled. Not that he hadn't considered it. As it was, he figured that Natasha's former lover—and murderer—had gotten off easy. If those cops hadn't shown up when they had, he might have ended up spending Mardi Gras in a Soviet prison, which would undoubtedly have been even worse than the chaos of this emergency room.

"Glad to hear that," his brother said equably. "How about the little story about someone trying to kill you?"

"That was, unfortunately, too true for comfort." Roarke sat down in an avocado-green molded-plastic chair and dragged both hands down his face as he remembered the fireball that had once been his car.

"Want to talk about it?"

There'd been a time when Roarke had been able to tell his older brother anything. From the nonjudgmental look on Mike's face, he figured that might still be the case.

"Probably. But not now." Not while the wounds were too fresh and raw.

"Suit yourself." Mike sat down beside his brother.

"I suppose the junior cop called you," Roarke guessed.

Mike laughed. "They just keep getting younger. Or we're getting older." It was his turn to sigh. "Now that's a damn depressing thought."

Although Roarke agreed, he didn't say anything.

"I think the cop got the story a little screwed up, though," Mike offered. "He said your wife was shot."

Roarke suddenly found himself on the uncomfortable proverbial horns of a dilemma. He'd never lied to either of his brothers. But if he told the truth, Michael would undoubtedly feel the need to get involved and until Roarke knew what, exactly, he was dealing with, he didn't want to risk anyone else's getting hurt. Even knowing Natasha had set him up to be killed that day, watching her die so horribly continued to weigh heavily on his conscience.

He knew that Natasha had left the hotel early to be out of the way. And because she hadn't known how Roarke was to be killed, it had been easy for Dimitri Davidov to make her the victim instead. Apparently, he had considered her even more of a threat than the American journalist. Which made sense, since it also turned out that Natasha had known a hell of a lot more about the crime syndicate than she'd told Roarke—things she'd apparently been willing to tell the western press for enough money, a long-term network contract and a one-way first-class ticket to America.

Knowing that he would never be able to forgive himself if he ended up getting his big brother killed, Roarke reluctantly decided to stick to the lie. For now.

"It's a long story. But yeah, that's pretty much what

happened. Looks like she got grazed by a random bullet."

"CNN didn't mention you had a wife."

"That's probably because nobody knew. We wanted to keep it quiet," Roarke improvised. "Until we could have a proper ceremony with friends and family."

"I see." Mike's tone remained deceptively mild. But Roarke knew he wasn't going to get away that easily. "When were you planning to tell Mom that she has a daughter-in-law?"

"That's partly what I came back to town for." Hell. The problem with lying was that you just kept getting in deeper and deeper. "To introduce her to the family."

"Is she Russian?"

"No. American."

"Where did you meet her?"

"This is beginning to feel a lot like an interrogation. So, when do you bring out the bright lights and rubber hoses?"

"I'm merely catching up on family news," Mike said evenly. "What's her name?"

Good question. And one the cop back on Rampart should have asked. Unless, Roarke considered grimly, the guy had already known the answer. Maybe he was one of the cops she'd been running from.

"Daria. Her maiden name was Shea."

He thought he saw a flicker of recognition in Mike's eyes, but it was gone too quickly to tell for certain. "Pretty name. Is she?"

"Is she what?" Roarke was beginning to feel more and more like a suspect. Although his brother had left the force over a year ago to set up his own private investigative business, Roarke figured once a cop, always a cop.

"Pretty."

The image of the clinging cat-suit she'd poured herself into flashed into his mind. "Yeah, but—"

"I know. You married her for her mind." Mike's grin was quick and wicked.

"So, how do you like your new career?" Roarke asked, wanting to shift the subject away from his alleged bride. "Are you living Thomas Magnum's high life with gorgeous women constantly throwing themselves at you?"

"Haven't had that much trouble dodging women. But I like the work just fine. Since I didn't want to spend the rest of my life peeking into motel-room windows in search of errant spouses, I decided to specialize in executive protection and company security. Unfortunately, times being what they are, I've got more business than I can handle."

"Sounds like you made the right choice, then." Roarke saw the double doors at the end of the room swing open.

"I think so." Mike's gaze followed Roarke's to the gurney the orderly was pushing. "That her?"

"Yeah." Roarke was already on his feet, making his way across the floor. He noticed he'd been right about the wound being merely a graze; the doctor had closed it with butterfly bandages. Her face was bruised from her hard landing on the pavement. "You're awake."

"Yes. I seem to be." She looked up at him. Then blinked. "Do I know you?"

Was she faking? Or did she really not recognize him? And if she was on the level, what else had she forgotten about this evening? As his brother came up behind him, Roarke couldn't decide whether to be relieved or chagrined by her apparent amnesia.

On the one hand, she wouldn't be able to prove him a liar. On the other hand, she also wouldn't be able to provide a lot of helpful information about what she was doing that had gotten her shot.

"I sure hope you do." He linked their fingers together, forced his expression into a concerned smile and lifted their joined hands to his lips to brush a light kiss against her knuckles. "I'm your husband."

"Husband?" She stared up at him uncomprehendingly, as if the word was unfamiliar to her. As if, perhaps, he'd suddenly begun speaking a foreign language. "We're married?"

"For better or worse." He managed a rough laugh. "And I have to say, sweetheart, let's hope that getting shot on your honeymoon is as bad as it gets."

"Honeymoon?"

"Mr. O'Malley?" An attractive Hispanic doctor came up to them.

"That's me." He took the hand she extended. "Roarke O'Malley."

"I know." The doctor's grin was quick and appealing. "I watch you all the time. I'm a fan.... I was just telling your wife that she's a very lucky woman."

"Far be it from me to argue, but I wouldn't call getting shot lucky, Doctor."

"Well, luck is relative, I suppose." She shrugged her white-jacketed shoulders, reminding Roarke that her working milieu provided, in its own way, as much violence as his own. "If that bullet had hit just a few centimeters either way, she could have been killed."

"Killed?" Daria's pain-laced eyes widened.

"It was an accident, darling," Roarke said quickly. Too quickly, he realized as he noticed his brother's all-seeing eyes narrowing. "Some Mardi Gras fun that backfired."

Appearing confused, she turned toward the doctor. "I can't remember anything."

"That's not unusual in a case like this, Mrs. O'Malley," the doctor assured her. "Although the wound isn't deep, memory loss is normal in the case of a head injury. Most everything should come back to you, in time." She smiled. "The trick is not to push it."

"Most everything?"

"There may be a few gaps. These things are always unpredictable." A flurry of activity across the room captured her attention. Glancing that way, Roarke saw a gurney being wheeled in through the emergency-vehicle entrance. A paramedic sat astride a man's supine body, pounding on his chest. "I'm sorry," the doctor said, "but I'm afraid I have to run." That said, she was gone.

"Well." Roarke looked after her. "Now what?"

"Your wife's going to be admitted," a nurse who suddenly appeared at his side answered. "For observation."

"I have to stay here?" Daria asked, clearly not pleased by the idea.

Roarke knew he was not imagining the fear that suddenly filled her eyes. Even if she really did not remember what had happened to get her shot, she knew she'd been in danger.

"It's just one night." Personally, he wasn't wild about the idea himself. "I promise to stay with you."

"There, you see?" the nurse said briskly. "We'll get

you into bed and by tomorrow morning, you'll be as good as new." She began wheeling the gurney away.

"We need to talk," Mike said as Roarke began to follow.

"Can't it wait?"

"No."

The tone didn't invite argument and Roarke was irritated by the way his brother was throwing his old cop attitude around. He forced a smile as he bent down and brushed his lips against a cheek that was as pale as paper. "I'll catch up with you in a minute, sweetheart."

Her only response was a faint nod.

"What's so important it can't wait until morning?" Roarke asked, turning to his brother.

Mike glanced around the crowded waiting room. "Let's go outside where we can have some privacy."

Frustrated, but undeniably curious, Roarke obliged.

"You're not married." Mike said when they were standing outside the building beneath the flashing ER sign.

"What gives you that idea?"

"The only ring your *wife* is wearing is an engagement ring."

"Maybe she lost the wedding band."

This latest round of questioning reminded Roarke of the time when he was ten and on a dare from Johnny Druen, had filched a Batman comic book from the Saint Charles Avenue Newberry's. When he'd discovered the petty crime, Mike had marched his brother back to the store, where he not only forced him to apologize and pay for the magazine, but also to agree to wash the windows and sweep the floors every day for a month.

"Maybe she didn't ever have one," Mike said grimly. "But that doesn't really matter. What does matter is the fact that you may have gotten yourself mixed up with a murderer, and I want to know what's up."

"A murderer?" Roarke found this statement impossible to believe. "That's ridiculous."

"You're staying at the Whitfield, right?"

"Yeah." Roarke folded his arms. "I suppose I shouldn't be surprised you found that out."

"I *am* a detective," Mike reminded him. "With enough of a pipeline to the cop shop to know that they found a body in a room at the Whitfield Palace Hotel tonight."

"Quite a coincidence," Roarke managed in a mild tone.

Once again he thought back to what she'd said about the cops wanting to kill her and wondered what his brother would say if he suggested such a possibility. Most of the New Orleans cops were guys like his brother, good guys trying to maintain balance in an increasingly dangerous world. But the police department also had its share of bad apples.

"But I sure as hell didn't kill anyone."

"Of course you didn't. You may have your faults, but even you wouldn't off some investigator from the Justice Department."

"The Justice Department?" Every nerve in Roarke's body went on red alert. Combine that information with Daria's deputy prosecutor's badge and they could be talking serious stuff.

"Yeah. Interesting thing, the guy wasn't registered as a guest there."

"He could have been using an alias. Or perhaps he

was visiting someone." Roarke didn't need a crystal ball to know what was coming next.

"Turns out he was. A woman. A woman who just happens to fit your bride's description."

Hell. It was happening all over again. Roarke wondered what unlucky star he'd been born under that destined him to keep getting mixed up with gorgeous, deadly females.

"Are you accusing her of killing a federal attorney?"

"If it turns out the dead guy was found in her room, she's going to have a lot of questions to answer."

Beginning with what she needed a hotel room for when her driver's license had revealed that she lived in town, Roarke thought.

"Maybe whoever killed the fed was after her."

"There's always that possibility," Mike allowed. "Particularly since she got herself shot. But with her claiming amnesia, it puts an interesting twist on the case."

"Now you're talking like a cop."

"And you're acting like a man with something to hide." Mike rubbed his square jaw. "Why don't you just come clean and tell me what you know?"

Roarke was relieved to finally be able to tell the truth. "Less than you. Hell, I didn't even know about the dead guy."

He went on to explain how they'd met. And how he'd lost her in the crowd, only to find her lying shot minutes later. And, more importantly, what she'd said about the cops wanting her dead.

"That's a serious accusation." Michael's expression was grim and cop-hard.

"I know. And she could be lying to cover her own

ass. But she was nearly unconscious when she told me that. I don't think she was alert enough to lie."

"Lying's second nature to some people."

"Got me there," Roarke agreed glumly, thinking of Natasha.

The first thing he had to do, he decided, was to get Daria Shea out of the hospital before the cops showed up, just in case she had been telling the truth back in the ambulance.

And then, amnesia or not, he was going to find out what kind of potentially fatal mess his mystery woman had gotten him into.

3

DARIA LAY IN BED, staring up at the water-stained ceiling, frustrated by the blank slate her mind had become. She tried to recall something—anything—about her life before she'd awakened in the emergency room, but all she could remember was noise and crowds and feeling afraid.

Of what?

Her hands were on top of the starched white sheet; she lifted the left one up, watching the way the diamond sparkled in the overhead light. He must have given her this, she mused. The man in the ER. The man who claimed to be her husband. The almost-overwhelmingly-large man with the thick shock of black hair and eyes the color of midnight over the bayou.

Ah. Her mind quickly latched on to that thought. She knew what the bayou looked like at midnight. Her mind conjured up another image of still water and trees draped in fog and Spanish moss.

"I wonder if I live there? With him?"

She pictured him again, his nose that looked as if it might have been broken more than once, and the lips that brought to mind a Celtic poet. Lips she almost could taste, making her believe that he might, indeed, be her husband. But when she tried to imagine them together in any family situation, her mutinous mind refused to cooperate and she drew another blank.

"Oh, God," she whispered, burying her face in her hands, "what am I going to do?"

Roarke stood in the open doorway looking at the pale despondent figure in the bed. He reined in his instinctive need to comfort, reminding himself sternly that getting involved with a gorgeous, mysterious woman had already nearly gotten him killed. He might not be the brightest guy ever plunked down on the planet, but he was damn well smart enough to learn from his mistakes.

He stiffened his resolve and walked into the room, closing the door behind him. "Was that the truth?" His need to remain absolutely uninvolved emotionally made the question come out harsher than he'd intended.

He watched her shoulders tense. She slowly lowered her hands and met his shuttered gaze with a wary one of her own. "Was what the truth?"

"That you can't remember anything."

His tone was thick with disbelief. Daria lifted her chin. "Why would I lie?"

Why indeed? Roarke thought. "How about the little matter of a dead man in your hotel room?"

"What?" Her eyes widened and although he would have thought it impossible, she became even paler. So pale, Roarke felt as if he could have put his hand through her face.

"The police found a dead federal attorney in a room at the Whitfield Palace. In a room reserved by a woman who is reported to be a dead ringer for you."

"I don't remember any hotel room," she insisted.

"And I definitely don't remember any man. Especially a dead one."

"That's what you say."

"Why would I lie about that?"

"Perhaps you killed him."

"Not on a bet. I'd never shoot anyone." That much she was sure of.

"Interesting that you know he was shot."

"Didn't you just say that?"

"Nope. I merely said a federal attorney was found dead. Period. No elaboration. No details."

Daria let out a long breath as she considered that damning statement. "How could that be? How could I know that a man was shot? And not remember?"

Good question. And one he intended to come up with some answers for. He crossed the room and stood beside the bed. "Let's start with your name. Do you remember that?"

Her brow furrowed. "The doctor called me Mrs. O'Malley." That hadn't felt right at the time and it still didn't.

Roarke decided to stick with his story until he got a handle on what she did or didn't remember. "That's right. You're my wife. Daria Shea O'Malley."

He waited for her to protest the name. Or to show some glimmer of recognition at the first part. But her expression revealed not a single sign that the name meant anything to her.

Daria repeated the name to herself, but it didn't stir any memories. She could have wept with frustration. "What's *your* first name?" she asked.

"Roarke."

"Roarke." The name didn't feel the faintest bit familiar on her tongue. Or to her ear. "Is that what I call you?"

"Most of the time." He shrugged. "Other times sweetheart or darling. And whenever I forget to pick the towels up off the bathroom floor, you're a bit more graphic."

His words and his expression were intended to make her smile, but Daria couldn't find anything humorous about her situation.

He'd just given her a hint of a domestic life. She tried yet again to picture them living together in conjugal bliss. Once again she came up blank.

"How long have we been married?"

"Not long." Another shrug.

"Well, that's certainly a help. Have we known each other long?"

Surely not. Daria couldn't imagine she could have forgotten such a forceful man. Forceful in a quiet sort of way. The kind of man one wouldn't want to cross. The kind of man who could protect a woman.

Where did that thought come from? Had she needed protecting?

"It was a whirlwind courtship. In fact, we decided to keep it a secret until I could get back to New Orleans and we could break the news to our families."

"Until you could get back... Does that mean I live here? And if it was a secret wedding, is that why I'm not wearing a wedding ring?"

"Yes to both questions, Mrs. O'Malley." If Daria was faking her amnesia, it was a damn convincing act, Roarke thought.

"But if I live here, why would I have a hotel room?" Her voice was a troubled whisper.

"I don't know, darlin'," Roarke answered quietly. "That's something we have to find out."

We. Daria wasn't sure why the word was so reassuring. She remembered nothing about this man...or a wedding.

She looked up at Roarke for a long, silent time. "You'd think I'd remember something as important as getting married."

"Yeah, you would, wouldn't you?" He leaned down, a wicked gleam in his eyes, his face inches from hers. "I've got to tell you, sweetheart, that one kind of hurts. You forgetting the honeymoon is turning out to be a real prick to my ego."

His smiling lips were nearly touching hers. All she needed to do was to lift her head off the pillow the slightest bit.

"I've kissed you." The startling realization that she knew exactly what those firm lips tasted like had her whispering the words out loud instead of keeping them safely in her head.

"That's a start." He wondered if kissing her again might stimulate her memory, and assuring himself that that was the only reason he was going to allow himself another taste of those satin-smooth lips, he lowered his head, closing the gap between them as she lifted her mouth to his....

"Sorry."

When the deep voice shattered the expectant silence, Daria pulled away, her eyes darting toward the door.

"Anyone ever tell you that you've got rotten timing?" Roarke growled, not taking his eyes from her.

"I just thought it might be good manners to welcome my new sister-in-law into the family," Mike said easily. "Before I leave."

Giving up for now, Roarke turned toward his brother. "Got a hot date?"

"Actually, I'm going to work. The owner of one of the riverboat casinos thinks his manager's skimming. I've been dealing blackjack all week." He held up his palms and smiled past Roarke to Daria. "You're looking at the fastest hands in the parish."

Feeling herself relax in the presence of this friendly man who looked so much like his brother, Daria returned his smile. "I don't know anything about gambling, but I think most women prefer a man with slow hands."

He laughed at that, a rich bold sound she knew had undoubtedly set innumerable feminine hearts fluttering. But as attractive and friendly as he seemed, as much as it warmed and relaxed her, it didn't affect her as much as a single look from the silent man standing by, watching them with more than a little interest.

"I'm Michael Patrick, the oldest and handsomest O'Malley brother. Welcome to the family." He came over to stand beside the bed, bent his head and brushed his lips against her bruised cheek. "Something tells me you're going to fit right in."

After the brief, brotherly kiss, he turned toward Roarke. "We need to talk again."

Fearing another interrogation, Roarke was about to refuse until he viewed the implacable determination in his brother's gaze. Although he'd been accused of being stubborn, there was not a man alive on the planet more tenacious than Michael Patrick O'Malley.

What had made him a great cop also tended to

make him a royal pain as a big brother, but Roarke realized he wasn't going to be able to dodge this lecture.

He turned back to his alleged bride. "Mike and I have some family business to attend to, then I'll be right back." He trailed a finger down Daria's cheek in what was meant to be a husbandly caress and experienced an unwelcome sense of satisfaction as he watched the color bloom in her too-pale complexion.

"Fine." For some reason she couldn't comprehend, Daria didn't want him to leave her alone. But not wanting to appear to be some clinging helpless female—even though she felt like one at the moment—she managed a faint smile. "I'm not going anywhere."

Not trusting her for a minute and determined that she not slip away from him again, Roarke went no farther than the hallway outside her door.

"Let me have it."

"What?"

"The latest big-brother lecture."

"Actually, I gave up trying to pull your fat out of the fire when you decided to defend Lila Comeaux's less-than-sterling reputation and took on the entire defensive line of the Sacred Heart High School football team."

"If I'd known she was giving it out to nearly every guy in school, I wouldn't have been so chivalrous," Roarke muttered, remembering how stupid he'd felt when Lila had bawled him out for beating up Billy Jones, the team fullback who, it turned out, had gotten her pregnant beneath the bleachers after the homecoming game.

"But Lila's old news," Mike said. "Updating our current story, I thought you might want to know that the murder in the city's most prestigious hotel is about to hit the airwaves.''

Roarke's curse was quick and ripe. ''Did you get that little bulletin from your pals at the cop shop?''

''No. This came from an old friend of mine. Désirée Dupree.''

''The reporter you were living with last time I was home?''

''Yeah, that's her. She ended up marrying another guy—a former prosecutor turned novelist—but we keep in touch.''

''I see.''

''You can wipe that smirk off your face, because we're just friends. Not every O'Malley brother is into hit-and-run relationships.''

No. Just he and Shayne fit that description. Mike had always been the responsible brother. Which wasn't all that surprising, Roarke considered, since with their father away so much of the time and their mother unable to handle three sons, Mike had been left to play the paternal role of disciplinarian while they'd all been growing up.

Given his upbringing, it was no wonder he'd become a cop. This way, Roarke figured, he could be big brother to the entire damn city. Or at least he had, until he'd gotten caught up in the juggernaut of political interests.

''What does the press know?''

''Only that a body was discovered in a room registered to a woman. Désirée got the impression that the cops have a pretty good idea who she is, but didn't want to share the information right now.''

''They could want to wait until they pick her up to

make the announcement to the press," Roarke mused. "Or they could be after her themselves."

Mike shook his head. "How the hell do you do it? A few hours in town and you've already gotten yourself mixed up in something dangerous."

"It's a talent." Although the circumstances certainly didn't warrant it, Roarke grinned. Then his expression immediately sobered. "Look, this is just between you and me, okay?"

A scowl moved across Mike's face like a thundercloud. "I should punch you for even having to think you'd need to say that."

"Sorry." It was the truth. "I guess I've gotten out of the habit of trusting anyone." That was definitely the truth.

"Join the club." Mike folded his arms. "So, what is it this time? And please don't tell me she's a defecting Russian spy."

"Nothing that glamorous. From the ID in her billfold, she's a deputy prosecutor."

"Daria Shea. I should have recognized the name." He didn't try to hide his chagrin.

"You know her?"

"Not personally. She got hired right about the time I quit the force. But I've heard about her. She's got a reputation for being brainy and unflinchingly honest, which is a real anomaly in this town. She's also reputed to be hardworking and willing to fight like a pit bull to put the bad guys away—no matter who they are. Which has ruffled more than a few feathers."

"Like down at the precinct?"

"There have been rumors of some ongoing investigations into graft and corruption," Mike allowed. "She's also busted a couple of judges for fixing traffic tickets, and another for being on the payroll of one of the drug gangs."

"A straight-shooting, aggressive prosecutor in this parish is bound to make a lot of enemies."

"I'd say that's an understatement." Mike paused as if wanting to choose his words carefully. "She also doesn't play the Southern-belle/steel-magnolia game like a lot of successful women do to ease their way in a male-dominated profession. In fact, now that I think about it, I've heard stories about guys getting frostbite just asking her out."

Thinking back to that heated kiss she'd initiated, Roarke decided his brother had to be wrong about that little bit of information.

"I don't suppose there's any chance of your going back to Moscow?" Mike asked.

"Not a one."

"How about paying a visit to the network offices in New York?"

"Nope." That was the last place Roarke wanted to be right now.

"Hell. I was afraid you were going to say that."

"I can't tell you what I'm going to do, Mike," Roarke said with honest regret, "because I want to leave you with plausible deniability, whatever happens. There's no point in risking your license."

"My license doesn't mean a thing compared to keeping my brother from getting killed."

"It's not going to come to that."

"I've heard that before."

"And I'm still alive."

"I know. And believe me, I consider that little fact proof that miracles do exist." He shook his head. "At least promise to keep in touch."

"Sure."

"Are you taking her with you?"

When Roarke only gave him a look, Mike shrugged. "Okay. None of my business. Got it." He took out a business card and a pen and scribbled a number on the back of the card. "This is my cell phone. Call me if you need anything. Anytime."

Roarke took the card and put it in his shirt pocket. "I will. Thanks. I've always said it was great having a big brother."

"And I've always said it was a pain in the ass having a kid brother who couldn't keep out of trouble."

The brothers hugged briefly, and in that fleeting moment Roarke understood why he'd come home. Family was a powerful magnet. Especially when your life had just come down around your ears.

"Would you do me one favor?"

"Sure," Mike answered promptly.

"Hang around here for about ten, fifteen minutes while I make a phone call and take care of a couple of things."

"Stand guard, you mean."

Roarke's expression was as serious as his brother's. "Yeah. I guess you could put it that way." He shot a quick, concerned look at the closed hospital-room door, then left to plan Daria's escape.

Twenty minutes later, Daria was looking at Roarke in disbelief. "You can't possibly expect me to wear that!"

He glanced down at the filmy harem outfit he'd bought from a ward clerk who'd quickly decided that spending the rest of her shift wearing a pair of green ER scrubs was definitely worth the hundred-dollar bill he was offering for her costume.

"It's not that bad."

Her scowl said otherwise. As she crossed her arms, he caught a glimpse of the hard-driving prosecutor Mike had described. Apparently the knock on her head hadn't altered her basic nature.

"It's nearly transparent."

"Not really. It's got this spangly bikini to keep you decent."

Her eyes narrowed as they raked over the glittery pieces of cloth he was holding out. "I may have lost my memory, but I'm positive that I'm not the spangly-bikini type."

Remembering what Mike had told him about her icy reputation, he figured she might just be right about that. However, frustrated that she was wasting precious time, but not wanting to blow even more time by getting into an argument, Roarke tamped down his temper and concentrated on his goal.

"It's Mardi Gras. Time to live dangerously."

"I'd say getting shot in the head was about all the danger I need for one night."

"Dammit." He dragged his hand through his hair. "Are you always this stubborn?"

She appeared unmoved by his frustrated outburst. She also seemed to be seriously considering his question. "I think I am."

"Terrific." No wonder people wanted to kill her. Much more of this and he would be tempted to wring her pretty neck. "Look, the cat-suit you were wearing when you were brought in is bloody—"

"I was wearing a cat-suit?"

"Yeah. And it fit like spray paint, which is why I don't see any reason for getting your panties in such a twist over this outfit. But, as I was saying, since you

obviously can't wear it, and I doubt you want to leave
the hospital in that lovely designer nightgown they
gave you..."

"No," she said quickly. "I'm one of those who believe air-conditioning made New Orleans livable, but
I'm not wild about air-conditioned clothing." She
frowned at the idea of her bare bottom exposed to the
breeze.

"Well, then, looks like you're about to join the
harem."

"If I live here, couldn't you just go to my home and
get some of my clothes."

"That's not an option. At least not at the moment. I
figure one of us getting shot in the head is enough for
one night."

She fell silent, her intelligent gaze taking in his grim
expression. "You're implying that my shooting wasn't
really accidental."

Roarke reminded himself that this was an intelligent woman who, despite her amnesia, would be able
to see through him in a minute if he tried to lie. "No.
Considering the circumstances, and that dead guy in
your hotel room, I don't think it was."

Her gaze dropped to the sheet. She traced random
circles on the white cotton as she thought over his
grimly stated words. "But why?" Her eyes were wide,
laced with pain and distress. "Who would want to
shoot me?"

"That's what we're going to have to figure out." He
held the costume out to her again. "After we get you
out of here."

Now that she had at least a partial picture of their
situation, Daria didn't hesitate. She plucked the harem
outfit out of his hand and pushed the sheet aside,

cringing only slightly as the movement caused the little man with the sledgehammer pounding away in her head to begin hitting harder.

"I'm not putting this on while you're watching," she said.

Roarke arched an eyebrow. "Hey, we're married, remember? I've seen you without clothes lots of times."

Daria was certain if she'd been naked with this man, she would remember it. "Get out of here, O'Malley. Call me crazy, but your wife has a sudden need for privacy."

It was the answer Roarke had expected. He wondered what he would have done if she'd been willing to undress in front of him.

"I'll be right outside."

The words, spoken with such authority, were more than a little comforting. Once again Daria thought how Roarke O'Malley, whoever he was, was a man capable of protecting a woman. And it seemed, for some reason, she was in dire need of protection.

Another thought—the most frightening thus far— flashed through her mind. What if the person she needed protection from was *this* man?

"What's the matter now?"

As she watched his eyes narrow, Daria realized that Roarke was a man who noticed every little nuance, heard things in voices most men wouldn't. Since she doubted that any woman would be able to keep secrets from such a man, that made him more than a little dangerous.

She opted for the direct approach. "How do I know I can trust you?"

"Good question." His lips twitched in a way that if

his eyes weren't so serious would have made her think he was almost smiling. "I could ask the same thing about you."

Roarke stood on one side of the railed hospital bed, looking at Daria in that shuttered, all-seeing way he had, and Daria stood on the other side looking back at him, caution warring with the need to believe him.

"Besides," he said finally, "you're the one who got us into this. I was merely sitting in the Blue Bayou Lounge, enjoying my first beer of the night, when you come out of nowhere and planted a kiss smack on my mouth."

"I knew I'd kissed you."

"You sure as hell did." This time he did smile. A bold, quick, unabashedly masculine grin that was the most dangerous thing about him so far. "And believe me, sweetheart, it was a humdinger."

For some reason, the idea that Roarke found her kiss pleasing—a "humdinger"—made Daria feel unreasonably pleased. "I suppose it's not unusual for a wife to kiss her husband."

"No." Roarke suspected she still wasn't buying that marriage story. "I suppose, since it's also our honeymoon, it's not that unusual for a husband to want to throw his wife down onto the dance floor and have his way with her, even if it does end up getting them arrested for indecent behavior."

"Arrested."

It was not a question, Roarke noted. She'd said the word as if it rang some far-distant bell. He waited with uncommon patience, practically seeing the wheels spinning around in her head.

"Damn." She closed her eyes and touched her fingertips to her temples, which were throbbing painfully. "I thought I had something." It had been there, like the remnants of a dream hovering on the fringes of her mind after wakening.

"Don't worry about it." He didn't admit that his frustration level was a lot higher than hers at the moment. "The doctor said not to push. The trick is to relax."

"Easy for you to say," she muttered in a way that made him laugh. "You find this situation funny?"

"Yeah. In an ironic sort of way." He shook his head as he thought about Yogi Berra's old chestnut. "You might say it's a case of déjà vu all over again."

The baseball great might have mangled the Queen's English. But no one could accuse the guy of not having a handle on human nature.

4

DARIA DESPERATELY WISHED the room came with a full-length mirror. From what she could see in the small poorly lit bathroom one, the costume was not what anyone hoping to go unnoticed would wear.

The diaphanous material in the Mardi Gras colors of gold, green and purple allowed glimpses of her legs in a way she feared was more suggestive than the briefest shorts. And the spangly top that looked like something worn by the dancers down on Bourbon Street, definitely gave new meaning to the name Wonderbra. She'd never dreamed she could possess such cleavage without a great deal of plastic surgery.

Although Roarke had told her she'd been wearing a cat-suit when she'd been shot, the combination of fascination and horror she felt viewing herself in the costume only underscored the feeling that her usual tastes were far more subdued.

She was wondering if she could tear the sheer sleeves off and somehow drape them across her breasts when there was a knock on the door.

"It's me," the now familiar deep voice said. "Are you decent?"

"That's a matter of interpretation." She sighed and surrendered to the inevitable. It was either this or the hospital gown, which was, of course, no choice at all.

"Don't you say a thing," she warned as Roarke entered the room. "Not a single, solitary word."

As if he could. Roarke was having enough trouble trying to keep from swallowing his tongue.

"And no leering."

"Whatever you say." Against his will, his eyes drifted toward those ivory breasts being presented to him like ripe pomegranates on a gold platter.

"Or looking."

He shook his head. "My mama, who was brought up to be a true flower of the South, did her best to raise all the O'Malley boys to be gentlemen. And I've tried to live up to her high standards. But I gotta tell you, sweetheart, you may just be talking about the impossible."

She drew in a deep frustrated breath, then realized her mistake when her breasts practically popped out of the gilt bra. "What is it about men that makes them prefer huge breasts over brains?"

"I don't know about most men. But personally, I've always thought any more than a handful was overkill. As for brains, vacuous, empty-headed females bore me. After all, most sex is between the ears."

Daria definitely wasn't in the mood to talk about sex. Not when his gaze was practically making her skin sizzle. "Did you say something about getting out of here?"

Her tone was frosty cool and haughty, at direct odds with her dressed-for-sin appearance, and the red flush that spread across her breasts like a fever belied the ice in her eyes. He had told the truth about preferring intelligent women; and even though he knew it was the most reckless, stupid idea he'd ever had,

Roarke was highly tempted to tumble her right here on that narrow hospital bed.

Tamping down the surge of desire, he concentrated on the immediate goal of keeping her alive until he could get his story and prove to the network brass that he wasn't the burnout victim they thought him to be.

"I'm ready if you are."

They left the hospital by a side door at the end of a narrow, dark hallway. Above the door a bright red sign warned that the exit was for authorized employees only.

"Won't it have an alarm?" Daria asked, looking up at the wires running along the top of the door.

"It did." He pushed the metal bar; the door opened with only the faintest squeak of hinges. "It doesn't now."

"I don't know whether to be impressed or appalled."

"It's an old system. Anyone could jimmy it."

"But not everyone would need to."

He took her arm and began walking across the parking lot. "You're the one who has people gunning for them, sweetheart. Not me."

What he said might be true, but Daria didn't like his patronizing tone. A temper she didn't know she possessed flared. "I'm so fortunate I have you to take care of me."

She wasn't particularly surprised when the sarcasm bounced off him without making so much as a dent. "You can say that again. Because you sure as hell weren't doing a real good job of taking care of yourself."

She might not know who she was. She might have the mother of all headaches and she might have been shot by someone for some reason she couldn't recall, but Daria was not the type of woman to simply let some sarcastic, overly macho male roll over her. Even if it appeared that he had saved her life.

Roarke went another two paces before realizing that she'd stopped dead in her tracks.

"What's the matter now?"

"I think this is where I tell you..." Her voice, edged with anger, drifted off. She literally swayed on her feet.

Even as he tightened his fingers, Roarke followed her gaze to the black-and-white NOPD squad car pulling up in front of the emergency-room doors.

"Come on." He put his arm around her waist and held her tight to steady her as he resumed walking. "I think it's time we blew this place."

He appeared to have a definite destination, which didn't surprise Daria. After all, he certainly seemed like a man who would always know exactly where he was going. When he stopped in front of a nondescript brown sedan, she was vaguely disappointed.

"Something wrong?" he asked.

"No. It's just not the car I'd picture you owning."

"That's probably because it's not mine." He opened the passenger door. "Hop in."

It could, of course, belong to someone he knew. But Daria didn't think so. "Are we stealing this car?"

"I wouldn't think a woman who'd just been shot in the head would be worried about petty crime."

Good point. "Still—"

"You know," he said mildly, "if you keep arguing, those cops are going to figure out you've skipped out on them and come looking for us. And although I like to think I can hold my own in a fair fight, I don't feel like taking on two armed policemen right now."

Daria stared up at him. "How did you—"

"You froze like a deer in the headlights when they drove up. Plus, you told me in the ambulance that the cops were trying to kill you."

"I said that?" As she did as instructed and climbed into the passenger seat, something stirred, like a ghostly image hidden in a veil of cold fog.

"Yeah." When he reached across to buckle her seat belt, his chest brushed against her breasts in a way that caused his mind to take an unwelcome detour.

He backed out of the car, shut her door, managing not to slam it, walked around the front of the car, opened the driver's door and threw himself into the driver's seat.

"Do you have a key?"

"We're going to have to improvise." He pulled the screwdriver he'd swiped from a maintenance man's toolbox out of his pocket.

"I don't think I want to know how you learned how to do that," she murmured, watching the way he used the screwdriver to punch the ignition.

"A guy tends to pick things up over time." The motor came to life. Although it wasn't the throaty lion's purr of his Porsche, it signaled good old American predictability. Which was exactly what he'd been looking for when he'd checked out the parking lot earlier. "You know the old Boy Scout motto: Be Prepared."

"And this is so much handier than lighting campfires or setting up tents."

He drove out of the parking place toward LaSalle.

"I've got to say this for you, sweetheart, you've got guts."

"I can't imagine you'd marry a woman who didn't."

Her earlier fear seemed to have been replaced by a cocky, never-say-die attitude he'd once felt himself. Once again Roarke thought that if she brought that same spunky tenacity to her work, it was no wonder someone was out to kill her. The surprising thing was that she was still alive.

"I assume you have a plan?" The traffic was lighter in this part of town, the tourists all seeming to have congregated in the Quarter.

"Never leave home without one."

His droll tone suddenly stirred a memory. A memory of this man in her living room. But he wasn't there in person, she realized. But on television.

"You're Roarke O'Malley."

"I already told you that."

"You told me your name. You didn't tell me what you did for a living."

"Most wives know what their husbands do," he countered mildly.

She'd watched him for years reporting from all the world's hot spots. Daria couldn't imagine forgetting being married to one of the country's most famous television journalists.

She was about to question that when he pulled into a long-term parking garage. "Don't tell me we're going to steal another car," she groaned.

"Don't have to." He drove up to the second level and pulled the stolen sedan into an empty slot. "I thought we'd pick up mine. I leave it here when I'm out of town."

It had been a year since he'd been back to New Orleans. Roarke could only hope the parking-garage attendant had kept the battery charged as he'd been paid extra to do.

"Won't the police be looking for it? After all, I doubt if there are many people in the ER who didn't notice you with me, and you did tell them all you were my husband, so why couldn't they simply run your name through their computers and—"

"You've been watching too much television," he interrupted brusquely. "We'll be okay."

Even as he reassured her, Roarke secretly admitted she had a point. If they could just get to the house, where she could rest and get her memory back, things would turn out okay. Which would be a nice change from Moscow.

Daria followed him to the elevator, which they took up to the sixth level. He walked halfway down an aisle, then stopped in front of a black Porsche.

"Being a world-famous journalist must pay very well," she murmured, thinking the low-slung car fit his personality. It was dark and dangerous.

"I do okay." They went through the car-door-opening procedure again. Daria's surprise at this gallantry made her think she wasn't used to having men open doors for her. When he looked inclined to fasten her seat belt again, she quickly forestalled him.

"I can do it."

He was already leaning into the car; their faces were just a few inches apart. All he would have to do is lean down just the least little bit and...

Damn! What was he doing, thinking of kissing a woman when half the bad guys in town were undoubtedly looking for them? There was something about Daria Shea, something that had caused a gut-stirring, red-hot arousal at the very time he needed to keep his cool. Angry at his lack of control and reminding himself that he must keep his head, he backed away. From the lady and from the potentially deadly attraction.

"Suit yourself."

He was furious. As she cast a cautious sideways glance toward him, Daria wondered what she'd done to make him angry. She certainly hadn't asked him to get involved with her life. Well, she admitted on second thought, if his story could be believed, perhaps she had.

Although it still didn't seem right to her that they were really married—yet why would he lie about that?—she had the feeling that he wasn't lying about her coming up to him in the bar and kissing him. Because, although she couldn't remember a single solitary thing prior to when she'd awakened in that noisy, blindingly bright emergency room, she had that hazy but blood-warming recollection of the taste of his lips.

"You know, you didn't have to leave the hospital with me," she said quietly.

"Yes, I did."

"But not because we're married."

He glanced over at her, took in her serious face and sighed. "No." His fingers tightened on the steering wheel. "Not because we're married."

"I didn't think so." Daria couldn't decide if she was glad about that or not. It was difficult to know what you felt when you didn't know who you were. "Why did you lie about us?"

"I figured it was the best way to make certain I could stick close to you until I got a handle on what was happening." He shrugged. "It seemed like a good idea at the time."

Daria thought about that. "It was nice of you to care."

"Don't romanticize things. I'm a reporter. I smelled a story." There was no softness in his tone. None of the kindness that she would expect from a man who'd gone to such trouble to rescue her. "Since I'm not working on anything at the moment, I figured I might as well follow it and find out where it led."

"I see." She didn't. Not really. But she did get his warning, loud and clear. There had been nothing personal in his behavior. And if she was foolish enough to think—or wish—otherwise, she would be disappointed.

Roarke made the tight left turn onto the third level, then cursed.

"What's wrong?" An instant later she saw the patrol car headed toward them and discovered that the old cliché about blood turning to ice was no cliché at all. "Oh, no."

"There should be a pen and a pad in the glove compartment," he told her. "See if you can find it."

Without asking questions, she leaned forward and did as instructed. "I've got it. Now what?"

"Hold on tight. And if you get a look at the number on that car, write it down."

He slammed his foot onto the accelerator, causing the Porsche to leap forward. For the next few seconds—although it seemed like an eternity—the squeal of tires reverberated from every concrete wall of the parking garage, adding a strident accompaniment to the runaway beat of Daria's pounding heart. Blue smoke and the smell of burning rubber filled her nostrils as the driver chasing them kept having to brake, the ancient domestic sedan not nearly as maneuverable as the sports car.

Roarke rocketed out of the garage, crashed through the black-and-white wooden barricade—to the obvious consternation of the openmouthed parking attendant—onto Lafayette, then jumped the divider and made another tight, tire-squealing turn on to Carondelet.

Although the police car followed, Roarke noted with interest that they had not hit their lights or siren—something that would be routine procedure under the circumstances.

Unless, of course, they were not acting as police officers, but as assassins.

There was a sound like a firecracker. Then the back window shattered. Roarke cursed, Daria screamed.

"Was that what I thought it was?" she asked shakily.

He gave her credit for being able to talk at all. "They're shooting at us," he confirmed. He felt the wetness on his face and suspected it was not caused by the rain that had begun to fall again.

When he wiped it away with the back of his hand, Daria leaned toward him. "You've been shot!"

"Naw. It's probably just glass."

"From a window the police shot out. Because they were aiming at me."

She couldn't believe it. What on earth had she done to deserve this? You would think she was some sort of deranged serial killer or something. She wanted to ask Roarke what, exactly, he knew about their situation, but decided this was definitely not the time. She only hoped she would live long enough to learn the answer.

The wide tires on the Porsche held the slick road, giving them an advantage over their pursuers. When a red Cadillac tried to pull out onto Carondelet from Saint Joseph Street, Roarke twisted the wheel and swerved, managing to miss hitting the passenger door. Unfortunately, the Cadillac driver's luck did not hold.

Looking back through the blown-out rear window, Daria watched in horror as the patrol car slammed into it, causing both cars to go skidding sideways over the center median.

"Too bad we can't stop and thank that guy," Roarke said about the Caddy driver as he continued on, around Lee Circle, headed toward the Garden District.

"You would have made it even without his interference."

Although he knew it was dangerous to like anything about this woman, Roarke decided he rather enjoyed the unwavering belief he heard in her tone.

"That goes without saying," he said with a shrug. But inside he was smiling.

"Oh, I got it," Daria said.

"Got what?"

"The number of the patrol car." She waved the piece of paper like a victory flag. "It spun around after it hit the other car and I saw the number painted on the rear, above the license plate."

A reluctant smile touched Roarke's lips. "Good girl."

She smiled back. And decided not to ruin the exhilarating mood by pointing out that his term was horribly chauvinistic.

Unlike the French-style houses in the Quarter, set flush to the sidewalk but boasting hidden courtyards in back, the magnificent mansions in the Garden District had been built back from the street in true American style, their lush green and flower-bedded front yards bordered by hedges, walls and fences.

Roarke stopped in front of a lacy cast-iron gate on tree-lined Prytania Street. The driver's-side window lowered with a faint whir. Daria watched as he leaned out the open window and punched a series of numbers into the box embedded in a brick pillar. A moment later the gate obediently slid open.

"Is this your house?" She stared in awe at the palatial house built in the eclectic blend of Greek Revival and Italianate styles that had been so popular in the booming South before the Civil War.

"Hardly. I may make more than your average news scribe. But even I couldn't afford this place."

"Then who..."

"It belongs to the government," he said as he paused between another set of pillars set on either side of the cobblestone driveway a long distance from the street. The electronic eyes scanned the car, then opened the overhead door to a garage that Daria figured could probably have housed the average new-car dealership showroom.

"The government?" The adrenaline rush from the car chase was beginning to wear off and her headache had intensified. "What does the government need with a mansion in New Orleans?"

Roarke pulled into the garage; the door closed behind him. "It's a safe house."

"Like in the spy novels?"

"Yeah, kinda."

"I thought you were a reporter."

"I am." He got out of the car, shut his door and came around to open hers. "It's my brother who's the spook."

This conversation was doing nothing for her headache. "Michael's a spy?"

She never would have guessed that calm and friendly man had such a dangerous occupation. Then again, she considered on afterthought, if a spy actually looked the part, he probably wouldn't ever be able to gather secret information.

"Not Mike." Seeing the pain in her eyes, he took her arm and helped her out of the bucket seat. "Shayne. He's the youngest O'Malley brother."

"You have a brother who works for the CIA?" The idea was incredible. How on earth had she gotten herself mixed up with spies and roving journalists and cops who wanted to kill her?

"Something like that." Roarke shrugged as he punched another code on the box beside the door leading from the garage into the house. "He's always been a little vague about what exactly he does. Which I guess makes sense, given his occupation."

"I suppose so." The door opened onto a wide double parlor, resplendent with soaring ceilings that appeared to be at least fifteen feet high and exquisitely carved moldings. A mural depicting life in the antebellum South had been painted on wallpaper that ran around the entire length of the room above the chair rail.

Daria drew in a quick appreciative gasp.

"Welcome to the house that cotton built," Roarke murmured.

"It's amazing." And also, save for the White House, undoubtedly the most expensive public housing in America. "I wouldn't be at all surprised to see Scarlett O'Hara dancing in Rhett's arms."

"Wrong state." In spite of himself, Roarke was impressed as well. "But right era. No wonder the government's running a deficit."

"Well, we certainly wouldn't want all those former communist spies and drug-dealing informants to be uncomfortable while they're being debriefed."

Her dry tone almost made him smile. Roarke decided it said something about Daria that she could try to make a joke at a time like this, after all she'd been through.

"Let's find the bedrooms," he said. "You look beat."

"I am."

Beat didn't even begin to cover it. Exhaustion didn't come close, either. What she was, Daria considered, was dead on her feet. She followed him across the gleaming mahogany floor, through the arched doorway festooned with plaster detailing, to a marble-floored foyer.

Daria almost groaned when she viewed the magnificent, curved double stairway. She guessed there must be at least thirty steps to the second floor.

Once again seeming to possess the ability to read her mind, Roarke scooped her into his arms and began carrying her up the stairs.

Feeling ridiculously like Scarlett O'Hara, Daria decided that she was a woman accustomed to standing on her own two feet. "I'm perfectly capable of walking by myself."

Like hell, he thought. "Shut up," he said instead.

"Excuse me?"

Icicles dripped from the words, giving him another glimpse of the woman Michael had accused of giving men frostbite.

"Look, so far tonight you could well have witnessed a murder, the bruises on your arms suggest that you've been attacked yourself, and you've been shot. I wouldn't think you'd be all that wild about ending the evening by falling down a flight of stairs and breaking your neck."

He had a point. But still, she didn't enjoy ceding control. Why, if she displayed half this weakness in court...

Court. The word rang an instantaneous bell. "Roarke!"

"What?"

"I think I'm a lawyer."

"Yeah. You are." He resumed walking up the stairs.

"Yeah?" She drew her head back to stare at him. "You knew?"

"You've got an ID card in your wallet that claims you're a deputy prosecutor for the parish."

"You've known that all along? And didn't tell me?"

Her accusing tone rankled. "Look, it isn't as if we've had a lot of time or opportunity for a long discussion. I figured we could talk about all this tomorrow. When you were rested and your head didn't feel as if some maniac was playing the anvil chorus behind your eyes."

"You should have told me," she muttered. "What else do you know about me?"

"What else?" He'd reached the landing. The carpeting was a rich plush burgundy, cream and navy Persian with such elaborate detailing Roarke figured an entire village must have gone blind tying all those intricate knots. "Let me think. I know your age from your driver's license—twenty-seven—and your weight—"

"That's not necessary," she murmured, leaning her head against his chest. She was so very tired.

"You don't wear corrective lenses, you live in the Irish Channel neighborhood—"

"I bought the house six months ago," she recalled. "It's a Victorian cottage. It reminded me of a little doll-house, but..."

"But, what?" he prompted when her voice trailed off.

"I don't know." She rubbed at her temple. "I seem to remember someone advising me against it, but I can't remember who."

"How about the guy who gave you that rock?"

She considered that, looked at the stone glittering on her finger and drew a complete blank. "Perhaps."

"Perhaps he's not from around here. Maybe he wanted you to relocate."

"That's a possibility." She sighed as the mental exhaustion returned. "This is obviously a dead end for now. How about something else?"

"Actually, there's not much left to tell. Except for your bra size, which is 34B."

"How on earth do you know that?"

"They gave me your bloody clothes at the hospital. Since I was your husband."

"Oh. But you already said that we're not really married." Her soft voice, which went up a little at the end of the sentence, asked him to please be honest about this all-important fact.

"No," he reconfirmed. "We're really not."

"Okay." That settled, she closed her eyes again and wondered why, if they weren't married, being in his arms like this felt so nice. And why she couldn't remember a single thing about a man she'd obviously promised to marry.

The first bedroom he came to was as elaborately decorated as the downstairs. Roarke pulled back the embroidered spread and laid her on the mattress of the four-poster bed.

She roused again as she felt the mattress against her back. "I can't sleep in sequins."

Personally, he thought she'd been doing a pretty good job of that already during those last few yards down the hall, but not wanting to start an argument, he merely pulled his black T-shirt over his head.

"What do you think you're doing?"

"Giving you my shirt. What did you think?"

Embarrassed color rose in her cheeks. "Never mind." She snatched the shirt from his outstretched hand and marched into the adjoining bathroom with more energy than he would have suspected she could muster.

"There should be toothpaste and brushes in the medicine cabinet," Roarke called in to her through the closed door. "Shayne said they keep the place pretty well stocked for unexpected visitors."

"I found them. Thanks." A toilet flushing. Roarke heard water running. Then, nothing.

He waited. Waited some more. Finally, beginning to worry that her head injury was worse than he'd been led to believe, he decided to forgo privacy to save her life. He knocked once—a hard, no-nonsense rap— then pushed the unlocked door open.

Daria was standing with her back against the wall, sound asleep.

5

ROARKE STOOD IN the doorway, looking at her. She was as pale as the shell-shaped porcelain sink and, engulfed in the black shirt that came down nearly to her knees, she looked small and frail and vulnerable.

He found the fact that she could sleep at all—let alone standing up—amazing. Then again, knowing all too well how depleted you could feel when the adrenaline rush faded, Roarke decided it wasn't all that surprising.

Had she been there when the Justice Department lawyer was murdered? he wondered yet again. Despite Mike's concerns, Roarke didn't consider Daria a suspect. Although he knew that appearances all too often proved deceptive, there was no way this woman was a cold-blooded killer. He would bet his life on that.

Which you've done before, a nagging voice reminded him. *And nearly lost.*

He shook off that depressing thought and reminded himself that his near-fatal relationship with Natasha Adropov was yesterday's ball score. Today was what counted. And what he had to do was figure out what exactly Daria Shea had gotten herself involved in that would have cops willing to kill a federal attorney, then come gunning for a prosecutor. Even a deputy one. Whatever it was, it was guaranteed to make a dynamite story. Headline news all over the country. Hell, it would probably get beamed around the world. The resulting fame would definitely shoot him right back up to the top of his profession, and Roarke wondered why the idea didn't give him as much pleasure as it once would have.

Perhaps Mike was right. Perhaps they were getting old.

Now that was a damn depressing thought.

Now that he thought about it, Roarke realized that he'd felt old when he'd stepped on that plane in Moscow, ancient when he'd landed in New York, and beyond even that by the time he'd checked into the Whitfield Palace. But that had been this morning, in what now seemed like another world, another time. Before he'd met Daria.

Drinking in the sight of those smooth, slender legs, Roarke felt that all-too-familiar pull of desire and reluctantly admitted that he wanted her. Who wouldn't? Brains and beauty were an appealing combination in any woman; toss in an extra helping of danger and he would be forced to worry about his masculinity if he didn't want to bed her.

But it went deeper than that, dammit. Beneath the journalistic curiosity and the male hunger, he felt an almost irresistible urge to protect her. The feeling, unbidden and unwelcome, made him all the more resolved to avoid entrapment.

Under different circumstances, he might have enjoyed tumbling the sheets with spunky, smart Daria Shea. Factor in the desire he'd witnessed in her wary gaze, and Roarke had no doubt that she would enjoy it, as well. But from the moment he'd found her lying facedown in a puddle at the feet of a cop who might have attempted to assassinate her, she'd become a story.

And that made her off-limits.

"Hey." He ran the back of his hand down her face. Her eyes flew open, her knees sagged, and if he hadn't caught hold of her she would have landed on the marble floor. "Wouldn't you be more comfortable in bed?"

"Bed." She sighed the word as if it were the most beautiful in the English language. "Yes." Her lashes drifted shut and she fell asleep again. This time in his arms.

The top of her head was just under his chin, and Roarke breathed in the scent of the hospital clinging to her hair. But beneath the antiseptic smell, he caught a faint whiff of that fragrance that, along with the enticing feel of her breasts pressed against his chest, caused another stir of forbidden desire.

He picked her up, carried her back into the bedroom, laid her on the mattress and covered her with a cotton sheet that was so finely woven it could have been spun from silk. Her hand, lying on top of the sheet, was bruised. He ran his finger over the purple mark; her skin was magnolia-soft and fragrant. He wondered if she smoothed that scented lotion all over her body, wondered if the man whose ring she was wearing enjoyed rubbing it on her back, her legs, her breasts....

Disgusted by the raw need that surged through him, Roarke dropped her hand, not gently, onto the mattress and resolutely turned away.

"Why don't you just strip yourself naked, tie a bunch of sticks of dynamite around yourself and walk into a convention of pyromaniacs, O'Malley?" he muttered as he left the bedroom. And temptation.

He had calls to make. A story to break. And then, he reminded himself, he could get on with his life as planned. Alone.

THE MOONLIT SPACE was unfamiliar, but Daria knew she was somewhere in the bayou. She was crouching in the shadow of a giant cypress, staring ahead of her in horror at the back of a young man. A rope around his neck was tied to a tree branch overhead; his feet dangled just inches above the ground.

Daria was aware of shadowy figures that seemed to be moving toward the hanging man. There was a hole in his chest large enough to put her fist into; through that gaping hole, she could see his heart, still alive and pumping blood. It spurted up like a geyser, drenching her in sticky red warmth.

And then she screamed.

Jerked out of a restless sleep, Roarke leaped from the chair and was at her bedside in a single long stride. She was sitting up, her eyes as wide, staring straight ahead at nothing. And screaming her head off.

"Daria." He ran an awkward, ineffectual hand down her hair. "Hey, it's okay." He patted her shoulder. "You were dreaming. It was only a nightmare."

He wasn't certain she could even hear him. Then, when the horrible sound coming from her throat suddenly stopped, he knew he'd gotten through.

"No." She shook her head, then looked up at him. Roarke watched as the confusion in her eyes changed to horror. "It was a nightmare." A sob caught in her throat; she drew in a deep, shuddering breath to clear it away. "But I wasn't dreaming. Not when it happened, anyway."

"When what happened?"

"The murder."

His fingers tightened on her shoulders. He relaxed them and forced a calm voice. "The one in the hotel room?"

She blinked, the confusion returning. "No. This happened in the bayou. They shot him."

Since Roarke didn't believe even the NOPD cops would risk detection by dragging a body back from the bayou and sticking it in Daria Shea's hotel room, he realized that they were now talking about two murders. And maybe more. Enough to bring a Justice Department investigator to town? Perhaps.

"Who was shot? And who did it?"

She opened her mouth. Then closed it. "I don't know. I don't recognize...the victim." She dragged a trembling hand down her face. "I don't understand why I can't see the others. I can see *him*. So clearly. Oh, God, too clearly."

When Roarke realized that he would do anything to banish the bleak frustration darkening her eyes, he knew he was in deep, deep trouble. Ignoring his vow to keep his distance, he sat down beside her on the bed and put his arm around her trembling shoulders.

"Don't be so hard on yourself. The doctor said some memory loss was expected. Besides, you just gave us another clue."

"What?"

"You said *them*. Obviously there was more than one person involved in the shooting."

She thought about that for a long, silent moment.

"You're right. They were wearing camouflage uniforms. And carrying shotguns."

A shotgun could make one hell of a hole in a man. Roarke wasn't surprised she was having nightmares.

"See? It's starting to come back. Just like the doc predicted."

"Not soon enough." She sighed and rubbed her temples. "I have the most excruciating headache."

"I'll get you something."

"How? We didn't stay around the hospital long enough to have anyone write us a prescription."

"I found some painkillers in the downstairs bathroom." When she looked up at him in surprise, Roarke shrugged. "I guess they're a standard item in the spy business."

Despite the pain it caused, Daria shook her head. "Your mother must go crazy with worry about her sons," she murmured. "Your brother the spy, you who spend your time chasing wars in all the world's hot spots, Mike..." She paused, obviously puzzled. "Did you say what Mike did for a living?"

"No." There had been a good reason for that. Knowing that she was just going to keep asking, Roarke said, "He's a detective."

She reacted precisely as he'd expected. "A detective?" Her voice was a mere sliver of shaky sound. "A New Orleans Police detective?"

"He used to be." His hand caressed her hair again in an attempt to ease her fear. "But he quit about the time you joined the prosecutor's office. He's gone private. Providing corporate security, stuff like that."

She belatedly recalled Michael having mentioned something about crooked casino dealers when they'd met, but she'd been so confused at the time, she hadn't really been paying attention.

"I was afraid—"

"I know." He ran the backs of his fingers down her face, avoiding the darkening bruise. "But Mike's one of the good guys. The best."

When she didn't immediately answer, he said, "You don't believe me."

"I do," she whispered. It was the truth.

"You shouldn't. You're not in any position to believe anyone. And you damn well shouldn't trust anyone."

She looked up at him, puzzled. "Are you saying I shouldn't even trust you?"

He laughed and Daria thought she'd never heard a sadder sound. "Especially not me." His voice was rough. His eyes dark.

She knew that she should distance herself emotionally from this man now, this very minute. She should break the compelling, almost-hypnotizing eye contact. That was, of course, what she *should* do. What any sane, sensible woman, especially a woman who was, apparently, a deputy prosecutor with a logical mind *would* do. Unfortunately, there was not a single logical thing about the way Roarke O'Malley made her feel.

Finally, unable to stand the way he was looking down at her, with those patient, unblinking, unemotional eyes, she swallowed and gathered up the scattered remnants of her composure.

"I suppose that would make us even, then," she said, with a detachment she was a very long way from feeling. "Because I get the impression that you don't trust me, either."

His answering smile was chilling. "Not on a bet."

That said, he stood. "I'll go downstairs and get you a pill."

He was at the door when she called out to him.

"Yeah?" He glanced back over his shoulder and felt a stir of complex and perilous emotions.

"Thank you." Her soft smile reached her pain-fogged eyes, turning them to amber. "For everything."

How did she do it? He was ten feet away from her, a distance that should have been safe, yet, as he looked at her sitting amid those tangled sheets, her hair tousled, Roarke felt himself being pulled into dangerous waters.

"You don't have to thank me." Steeling his heart against an involvement he couldn't afford, he made his tone purposefully gruff. "I'm a reporter, remember. And you just happen to be the best story I've stumbled across in months. You're also my ticket back to the big time."

Bull's-eye. The soft flush drained from her face as the brusque shot hit its mark. He watched her teeth bite into lips that had begun to tremble.

You're a son of a bitch, O'Malley, he told himself as he turned back and continued out of the room. As he walked down the ridiculous *Gone with the Wind* staircase, he assured himself that he'd done the right thing. The only thing possible. The attraction that had sprung up between them from the beginning was as dangerous for her as it was for him.

If he was to keep her alive while he unearthed the truth about what had happened to her, he would need a clear head, a cool mind. If he allowed himself to be distracted by her not-inconsiderable charms, they could both end up dead. And if he found himself forgetting to keep his distance, all he had to do was remember the last time he'd played Sir Galahad to a female in distress.

Daria watched him leave the room, then turned her head into the fluffy down pillow. She was confused and frustrated, scared and angry. And although she knew, with ever fiber of her being, that she was not the type of woman to find dark, dangerous men the slightest bit appealing, she was shockingly, disturbingly attracted to Roarke O'Malley.

"He's right," she muttered. "You can't trust anyone. Including him." And even though she'd already made the mistake of trusting him with her life, she was determined to keep her heart to herself.

The thing to do, she decided, was to use him to help her find out what case she'd been working on that had almost gotten her killed. As a reporter, he was accustomed to digging out stories. And what facts he couldn't unearth, perhaps his brother, the cop-turned-private-detective, could.

She would use Roarke O'Malley just as he claimed to be using her. And if everything turned out all right in the end—and she could not allow herself to believe it wouldn't—she would get to put some murderers behind bars and he would get an exclusive on a dynamite story.

Then, after they'd both gotten what they wanted, she could get on with her life. Alone.

"Well, not exactly alone," she murmured, glancing down at the ring that was glittering like ice in the slanting silver moonlight streaming into the room.

Why was it, she wondered yet again, she had no memory of the man she'd promised to spend the rest of her life with? She suspected that if Roarke were her fiancé, she wouldn't have forgotten him for a moment.

Unwilling to dwell on that disturbing thought while her head was pounding, she closed her eyes and drifted back to sleep.

THERE WERE DEFINITELY advantages to being a war correspondent. Accustomed to sleeping on planes, trains, camel caravans, and on the hard ground with rockets streaking overhead, Roarke had no trouble catching a few zzzs in the chair beside Daria's bed. She'd been asleep when he'd returned with the Percocet and reasoning that it probably wasn't all that wise to take medication with a head injury anyway, he hadn't wakened her.

He could have claimed a bed in one of the other rooms, but again, because of her head wound, he didn't want to risk leaving her alone all night. He slept lightly, aware of the traffic outside on the street—he'd almost forgotten how this city never slept—the creaking sounds of the hundred-and-forty-year-old house settling down for the night, the occasional tapping of the rain on the roof, the bark of a dog in the distance and the whistle of its owner as it was summoned back into the house.

It was a little before dawn when he woke, amazingly refreshed considering that he should still have been suffering from major jet lag. Adrenaline, he thought. Not the jolt that comes from danger, like last night's high-speed chase, but the energizing feeling he always got when working on a hot story.

Using the bathroom down the hall, he showered, shaved, then checked out the clothes Shayne had assured him he would find in the closets. A look at the selection revealed that spies came in almost all sizes. But unfortunately not his. He did find some silk boxers that not only fit, but felt damn good against his skin, and a cashmere sweater that was too snug, but since Daria was currently wearing his T-shirt, it would have to do.

"Beggars can't be choosers," he recalled his father saying on one of his infrequent visits home. Not that any beggar Roarke had ever run across sported cashmere.

As he pulled on his black jeans, his stomach rumbled, reminding him that he hadn't had any dinner last night. He would have breakfast, then figure out a plan. Maybe Daria would wake up this morning with more of her memory restored. Feeling more enthusiastic than he had in a very long time, Roarke went off in search of the kitchen.

THE SMELL OF COFFEE drifted into Daria's consciousness like wisps of fog along the levee, teasing at the ragged edges of the dream from which she could not escape.

She was in the bayou again, running as fast as she could across the trembling ground, her blood pounding in her ears, her breath coming in deep, burning gasps that were literally ripped from her lungs.

If the men with the shotguns discovered her, they would kill her. Then they would throw her body to the alligators.

The full moon created streaming silver ribbons of light and deep purple shadows that appeared to hang from the ancient cypress trees like Spanish moss. She tried to stay in the shadows, but from time to time she would have to race across a clearing, knowing that she might as well have been running through a spotlight.

She tried to stay calm; the bayou was a haunted maze that a person could enter and never escape from. Like that man lying back there on the ground, with a fist-size hole in his chest.

An owl screeched, sounding like a woman in pain. Dogs were baying; she worried they might be bloodhounds sniffing out her trail. Her legs were trembling; forcing them forward became more and more difficult. Just when she was certain she couldn't run another step, she slammed into a fallen tree trunk and went sprawling. As she struggled to push herself to her feet, she saw the cars parked along the dirt road.

She half crawled, half walked to her red convertible and pulled her keys from her jeans pocket.

Her hands wouldn't stop shaking. She tried again and again and finally managed to get the door open and crawl into the driver's seat. Then her hand was trembling so badly she couldn't stick the key into the ignition.

Finally, she succeeded. She pulled the lever for the parking brake and put the car into neutral, hoping it would roll a safe distance away. But the land was as flat as a billiard table, and it drifted less than three feet before coming to a stop. She was forced to start the engine.

It roared to life with a noise that seemed deafening. Her pursuers would be sure to hear it. She shifted again and began driving toward New Orleans as fast as she could. As she drove, the image of what she'd witnessed flashed through her mind in all its gory detail. Bile rose like acid in her throat as she was forced to picture that dead man; forced to acknowledge the horrifying fact that her worst fears had been realized.

She pulled over to the side of the empty two-lane country road, got out of the car, fell down on her knees and began retching into a stand of tupelo.

Finally it was her own coughing that woke her, dragging her from the painful nightmare. Daria looked around the room in confusion, at first not recognizing the magnificent antique hand-carved bed, the damask-covered walls topped with crown molding, the windows draped in gold-and-burgundy brocade.

And then she heard the murmur of voices drifting up the stairs, realized it was coming from a television, and the night before flooded back. She remembered her arrival at this luxurious mansion, the chase through the darkened night streets, her hospitalization, and most vividly, running into the Whitfield Palace's Blue Bayou Lounge and kissing Roarke O'Malley.

Okay. So, if she could remember all that, why couldn't she recall what she'd been doing *before* she'd dashed into that cocktail lounge?

"The doctor said not to push it," she muttered as she climbed out of bed. "Easy for her to say."

Although she'd worn it all night, the T-shirt still smelled like Roarke—a dark, masculine scent that stirred feelings she was better off not thinking about.

"Whatever happened, Roarke O'Malley is a complication," she reminded herself firmly as she locked the bathroom door. "One you don't dare risk."

With that warning ringing in her mind, she stepped into the shower and took advantage of the shampoo, conditioner and liquid soap in the Lucite dispenser beneath the shower head. The needles of hot water drumming against her skin felt like heaven; she tilted her head back, allowing the streaming water to wash the lingering disinfectant odor down the drain along with the fragrant lather.

She wrapped a fluffy white bath sheet around herself, then found the toothbrush and toothpaste she could just barely recall using the night before. She brushed her teeth, picked up the silver-backed brush and dragged it through her thick wet hair.

She was debating searching for a hair dryer when she suddenly became aware of another scent, more enticing than the shampoo and even more stimulating than Roarke's T-shirt.

She exited the bathroom and came face-to-face with him standing beside the bed, arms folded as if he'd been waiting for her.

6

ALTHOUGH SHE KNEW she was not accustomed to greeting men she hardly knew wearing only a towel, the thick bath sheet effectively covered her from her breasts to nearly her ankles, which was a great deal more than either that ridiculous harem outfit or Roarke's T-shirt had done. That being the case, she refused to reveal any embarrassment. She also decided to ignore the flash of desire in his indigo eyes.

"Is that bacon I smell?"

As he took in the sight of her wet and nearly naked, Roarke had to remind himself yet again that bedding Daria would be the second-biggest mistake he'd ever made. "And *pain perdu.*"

She couldn't remember the last time she'd indulged in the delicious local treat of French toast made with French bread.

"I think I've died and gone to heaven."

"That's what we're trying to avoid." He took a robe from the back of the chair. "I found this in a closet. Although you look damn good in that towel, I think it might offer a bit more temptation than I'm capable of handling at the moment."

"You sound as if I don't have a choice about what might happen."

"Ah, but that's part of the dilemma, darlin'." Despite the still-treacherous circumstances, despite the fact that just looking at her all wet and flushed had sent the blood roaring from his head straight into his groin, where it pooled, hot and thick, Roarke was feeling uncharacteristically upbeat. "You *do* have a choice. And from the way you kissed me last night..."

Believing that the best defense was a strong offense, Daria lifted her chin. "I have no intention of sleeping with you."

He had the audacity to smile at that. A roguish grin that slashed white in his dark face and made his eyes gleam like sapphires. "Well, if you insist on splitting hairs, I think this is where I admit that sleeping wasn't exactly what I had in mind."

Shaken by the sexual awareness that hummed through her veins at the merest look or touch from Roarke, she willed her voice to chipped ice.

"Fine. Then let me be a bit more specific so you can understand. I'm *not* going to have sex with you."

It was the same thing he'd been telling himself all morning while he'd been rattling around the kitchen, thinking of her lying up here all warm and soft, wearing nothing but his T-shirt. It was safer that way. Unfortunately, as he was struck with a sudden urge to lick those beads of moisture off the crests of her ivory breasts, Roarke remembered than he'd never been a real fan of *safe*. It was, after all, a close cousin to boring. Unfortunately, lust fogged the brain and caused a man to take foolish risks.

"I suppose, then, I'll let you get dressed."

"Thank you." She plucked the robe from his outstretched hand. Their fingers briefly touched, creating a spark that shot straight to her bare toes. He was a testosterone bomb and whenever she was around him, Daria could feel the radiation burning through her. She glanced up into his face to see if he'd felt it, too, but his features were set into a smooth, unreadable expression.

When the phone on the bedside table rang, she jumped.

"That should be Mike. He promised to call me back." Roarke scooped up the receiver.

"Yeah? Great, I'll meet you at Monkey Hill in thirty minutes." That said, he hung up.

The brief conversation told her nothing. "Why are we going to the zoo?"

"*We're* not."

"But—"

"*I'm* going to the zoo. *You're* staying here." When she opened her mouth to argue, he pressed a finger briefly against her lips. "In case you haven't noticed, you don't have the wardrobe for a day in the park." Roarke trailed the wicked finger along the top edge of the towel, just centimeters from her skin. "Unless you feel like joining the harem again."

"That wasn't on my list of things to do today."

"I didn't think so." He admired the way she seemed determined not to let her situation overwhelm her. He knew lots of women—hell, even men—who would have been basket cases about now. "So, I'm meeting Mike, who has already retrieved my luggage from the hotel, then we're going over to your house and get some of your stuff."

"Isn't that dangerous?"

"Naw. You're talking about the O'Malley brothers. We can take care of ourselves," he added as he watched the color begin to fade from her cheeks.

"So, you've got about twenty-five minutes to make a list of what you want out of the house, if you can remember what's there, and eat *pain perdu*, which is undoubtedly turning to roofing shingles in the warming oven."

Shoving his hands deep into his pockets to keep them out of trouble, he left the bedroom.

"THIS IS DELICIOUS." The French toast was golden brown, smothered in melted butter and syrup. "I never would have suspected you'd be a man who knew how to cook."

"Since eating isn't exactly an optional activity, I figured I'd better learn."

"I'm surprised." She took a sip of sweet, rich café au lait. The small television on the kitchen counter was tuned to a local morning-news program. At the moment, an attractive blonde in a red jacket and a short, amazingly tight skirt was pointing out high-pressure areas on a Louisiana map.

He eyed her over the rim of his cup. "Why?"

"You seem like a man women cook for."

"There are a great many things I'd rather have a woman do for me than cook."

When his eyes took on that devilishly seductive gleam again, Daria looked away, dragging her attention back to the television.

"Oh, my God." Recognition came crashing down on her.

"What?" Roarke immediately abandoned the idle fantasy of taking her on top of the kitchen table and followed her gaze.

"It's James."

Although Roarke had rarely been in New Orleans these past years, he would have had to have been covering wars on Mars and Jupiter not to immediately recognize the man whose handsome face was filling the small screen. James Boudreaux had begun his political career as a Jefferson Parish prosecutor, earning an unprecedented ninety-eight-percent conviction rating. Needless to say, a citizenry obsessed with rising crime subsequently rewarded the apparent hard-liner on crime with a U.S. congressional seat. Now rumor had him eyeing the bigger—and more stable—prize of a senate seat.

Roarke wondered if those same voters would be so eager to show up at fund-raising dinners if they knew his reputation among hardworking, often-beleaguered cops who grumbled that he only took on cases he was guaranteed to win, thus sending a great deal of scum right back onto the streets. Which, of course, raised crime rates, which in turn made Boudreaux's law-and-order political stance even more popular.

He pointed the remote at the television screen, increasing the volume.

"Of course, it's a black eye on the city any time a murder occurs," the congressman was saying.

Although his grandfather had been a struggling Cajun rice farmer, no trace of the bayou remained in Boudreaux's deep, cultured voice. The charcoal-gray suit was Italian, the burgundy tie was silk, and discreet gold links flashed on snowy white turned-back cuffs.

"The fact that the victim happens to be a federal attorney admittedly draws more attention to the crime, but the death itself is no more tragic than the loss of any other citizen."

"I think I hear a speech coming," Roarke murmured, wanting to mute the sound, but needing to hear what officials were telling the press about the man who'd been murdered in Daria's hotel room.

"James is never one to miss an opportunity to wax elegant," Daria said dryly. "Especially when it results in campaign contributions."

"Sounds as if you know him well."

"I do." She sighed and listened as he went on to offer condolences to Martin Fletcher's widow and children. She looked down at the diamond solitaire that was catching the morning light and splitting it into rainbows that danced on the walls and ceiling. "He's my fiancé."

IN A FEDERAL reproduction home located in the heart of Alexandria, within walking distance of the Potomac River, James Boudreaux paced the antique Persian carpet of his library. He was more furious than he'd ever been in his life. And, dammit, for the first time terrified that everything he'd worked for, all he'd fought for in his entire life was about to come tumbling down around his ears.

"How the hell could they let her get away?" he demanded, turning on the man who'd reluctantly broken the bad news.

"They almost had her. If Roarke O'Malley hadn't come along when he did—"

"O'Malley." Boudreaux spat out the name as if he'd taken a bite of bad crayfish. "He and his brothers have given me nothing but trouble for years." His jaw hardened; his pale gray eyes turned to chips of steel. "Tell them that when they find my fiancée and her knight errant, I want them to make certain they don't get overenthusiastic and kill him."

Pale eyebrows arched. "You want them to leave O'Malley alive?"

"Only until I get there. This is one execution I'm looking forward to performing myself."

"Yes, sir."

Boudreaux lit a thin black cigarette with a silver lighter, then glared out through the exhaled cloud of blue smoke.

"What the hell are you still doing here?" he demanded. "The longer it takes to find them, the more damage that bitch can do. And believe me, if she takes me down, I won't be going off to Angola alone." The idea of ending up in that hard-time prison with crack-heads, rapists and common murderers was enough to chill his blood. And harden his resolve.

"Call them back and tell them I expect results. And book a seat on the first flight to New Orleans."

"Yessir." The aide hurried away to follow instructions. He didn't see the congressman from Louisiana slump down into the glove-soft cream leather chair behind his desk. Didn't see him drag his hand down over his face, or pick up the Waterford replica of the Capitol Building Daria had surprised him with after the election.

"Goddammit!" Boudreaux threw the gift against the stone fireplace, where it shattered into hundreds of crystalline pieces.

"I DON'T UNDERSTAND," Daria said, breaking the suffocating silence that had surrounded them since Roarke had turned off the television. She leaned forward and pressed her fingertips against her temples, feeling more confused and frustrated than ever.

"How can I remember being engaged to James and

not remember what I was doing in the Whitfield Palace Hotel?"

"The doc said head injuries are unpredictable." The nagging little suspicion that she might be lying raised its head again. "Let's see what we've got so far. You remember being engaged to James Boudreaux."

Her memory jogged, kicking out another piece of the puzzle. "For six months." She looked up at Roarke in surprise. "I just realized that."

"See, it's all coming back. And you remember being an attorney."

"I have a hazy image of arguing in court. But I can't pin down any cases."

"One step at a time. And you vaguely remember kissing me...."

An image flashed in Daria's mind—an image of Roarke dressed in a bomber jacket, black T-shirt and jeans, standing out like a beacon amid the costumed Mardi Gras celebrants. She also recalled the woman who had been practically crawling into his lap.

"You looked like a man who needed rescuing."

She watched as his eyes turned dark and almost hypnotic. "You felt a need to rescue me?"

"That silicone-enhanced blonde was definitely a barracuda."

Roarke caught the edge underlying her tone and wondered if she could possibly be jealous. The idea, which should have sent him running in the opposite direction, proved strangely appealing.

"Nothing dangerous about you, sugar." His deep drawl took the edge off his sarcasm, even as it set all her nerve endings vibrating again. He leaned back in his chair and took another long drink of coffee. "Okay. So you now obviously remember coming into the Blue

Bayou Lounge. Want to try for what went on upstairs in your hotel room?"

"It couldn't have been my room," she insisted. "Why on earth would I need a hotel room, when I already have a house in town?" She paused and frowned. "Are you suggesting that dead Justice Department attorney...that Martin and I were..." Her voice trailed off.

"I don't know what you were up to in that room. But according to Mike, who's got some informants at NOPD, you bear a striking resemblance to the woman who booked it two days ago. It'd be my guess, what with all that's happened, that you'd booked it for some reason."

"Do you happen to know if I—she—paid by credit card?"

"Cash."

"Oh, God." She closed her eyes and pressed her fingertips tightly against them, as if she could force the swirling colorful lights behind her lids to form into a coherent, visible image. "I hate this."

He watched with admiration as she fought for composure. "Hey, maybe it wasn't you at all. Or maybe you were just having a wild fling with the guy and ended up in the wrong place at the wrong time."

"He's married."

"So? Not all women care about little niceties like that. *You're* engaged," he reminded her succinctly.

"If we *were* having an affair," she mused, "his wife could have followed him to New Orleans. *She* could have been the one who shot him."

"That's one scenario."

An unsavory thought swirled up from the fog cloaking her mind. "What if I was the one who shot him?" Her voice was thin and ragged, her eyes wide and more frightened than they'd appeared when she'd realized someone might have been trying to kill her.

"You didn't."

"How do you know?"

"I just do." His instincts were telling him she didn't have it in her to murder anyone. Then again, the faint voice of reason in the far reaches of his mind counseled that his instincts had been wrong before. Dead wrong.

"Because I'm a good kisser?"

He looked at her in mock surprise. "Did I say that?"

His words had the desired effect, bringing color back into her ghost-white face and a flash of gold fire to her eyes. "'A humdinger,' I believe, was how you so colorfully put it."

"I believe you might be right. Want to try again? See if we can make world-class?"

She was too tempted. Her lips went dry. "I don't think that would be a very good idea," she said reluctantly.

"On that we're agreed." He sighed heavily and pushed himself out of the chair. "I've got to leave. I'm going to be late meeting Mike as it is. Anything specific you want me to get at your house?"

Daria nodded. "I was able to make a list." She was pulling a folded paper from the pocket of her robe when a sudden thought stopped her. "You're still going?"

Roarke leaned over and deftly pried the paper from her fingers. "That was the plan," he reminded her.

"But everything's changed."

"Nothing important."

"But now I remember finding Martin's body in my hotel room."

"But you don't know what he was doing there in the first place. Or who could have shot him."

"True, but—"

"Which means that you're still a sitting duck. And I'm not going to take a chance on anyone getting a second shot at you."

"I'm not accustomed to anyone making my decisions for me."

"Ah, but I'm not just anyone. And perhaps if you'd let someone else in on whatever you were up to, you wouldn't have ended up in this mess in the first place. However, now that you have," he said, ignoring her quick intake of angry breath, "someone's got to keep you alive long enough to solve this crime."

And for some reason, she'd chosen him to do it, Daria reminded herself. He certainly hadn't asked to be dragged into her troubles.

"You seem to be forgetting one thing," she said.

"What's that?"

"James is an important man. He can protect me."

"Yeah, he was doing a bang-up job of it yesterday. And before you open that sexy sweet mouth to argue that he might not even know about your involvement in the case, believe me, sweetheart, the cops know damn well who the mystery woman in the hotel room is. Which means Boudreaux knows, too. And you notice that he didn't make a single reference to his beloved fiancée being missing."

"Perhaps he didn't want to tip his hand and ruin the case or risk endangering me if I'd been kidnapped. Perhaps he's tried to call my house—"

"The only message on your recorder is from the tailor at the dry cleaners, telling you that the alterations are finished on your new suit."

"How on earth do you know that? You haven't even been to my house yet."

"Dick Tracy Crime Stoppers tip for today, darlin'— If you don't want crooks to rob you blind, you shouldn't write down your ATM PIN number, your burglar-alarm code and your voice-mail retrieval number all on the same card in your wallet."

"I used a code," she muttered, reluctantly admitting to herself that he had her there. Wasn't her own office constantly printing up pamphlets warning people of that very thing?

"Yeah. It was real clever replacing the numbers with letters. I hate to shatter your James Bond fantasy, but most kids learn that particular secret code by the time they're in Cub Scouts."

Having no argument to that, Daria returned to the one thing he'd said that was too ridiculous to be believed.

"Did I misunderstand, or did you just accuse James of being a suspect?"

"As my brother Mike would say, 'At this point, everyone's a suspect.' Including your pretty-boy fiancé."

"But not me?"

Roarke decided to be brutally honest in order to keep her from sneaking out of the house while he was gone. "I've got a gut feeling you don't have it in you to kill anyone. But I'd also be willing to bet the cops don't share my opinion. You go out on your own and you could end up getting arrested. And that would be the *best-case* scenario."

He didn't have to remind her what the worst would be. As the memory of her assailant flashing his badge at the kids in the cemetery flashed all too vividly through her mind, Daria realized she'd already gotten a taste of that one.

"I won't go anywhere." The headache had begun throbbing behind her eyes again.

"Good girl. And although it *should* be safe, don't answer the phone, either." He was almost to the door when he snapped his fingers and stopped. "Damn."

"What's wrong?"

"I forgot something." He came back to stand over her, forcing her to lift her head to look up at him.

"What?"

"This."

He bent down, caught her chin between his fingers and covered her mouth with his.

The moment his lips touched hers, Roarke belatedly realized he'd dived into a tidal wave.

He was drowning. Drowning in her sinfully sweet taste, in her deceptively innocent scent, the feel of her warm female body against his, the soft little sounds she was making deep in her throat. He'd always been a man who had looked for adventure, who had enjoyed living on the edge, but not even in Moscow had his need for excitement threatened to lead him into such peril.

He'd thought he'd known passion, but as Daria's eager mouth softened beneath his, Roarke knew he'd never even come close.

She wanted him. He could taste it in the hungry way she was kissing him back—like a woman who'd been starving and had suddenly stumbled across her own private banquet.

Roarke wanted her. Recklessly. Dangerously. Damned near beyond reason. With a hunger that went deep into the very marrow of his bones. And even though he knew it was reckless, he was tempted to take what he wanted. What she was obviously so willing to give.

Sex was just sex, he reminded himself. Lust was easily satisfied in his world, if not with one woman, with another. So long as he kept his emotions in check, so long as he didn't allow himself to care about Daria Shea, he wouldn't have to worry.

Even as he assured himself of that, Roarke's blood began to swim. He felt like a man going under for the third and final time. If he didn't manage to pull himself to the surface, right now, he would surely drown.

She didn't know this man, Daria reminded herself as she linked her fingers together behind his neck. Not really. A sensible woman would keep her distance, protecting herself as best she could until she could remember the truth.

But dear heaven, what in the world was a woman to do when, with a single glance of those hooded midnight eyes, he could make her knees weak? And when the powerful force of his mouth literally took her breath?

At this moment, alone with him in a house that was proving anything but safe, there was no right. No wrong. Only this reckless, unrelenting need.

The faint little whimper of protest as he lifted his mouth from hers almost had Roarke reconsidering his decision to try to back away. Now.

He shook his head, like a diver who'd been underwater too long and had surfaced too fast.

Then, before Daria's whirling head had cleared, he was gone, leaving her more confused than ever. And wanting.

7

MONKEY HILL, LOCATED near the banks of the Mississippi, had been constructed so the children of New Orleans could see what a hill looked like. The pavilion on the bank was one of the best places from which to view the river and it was there Roarke found his brother waiting.

"Sorry I'm late. Something came up."

"Something to do with your mystery woman?"

"Sort of. She just remembered she's engaged to James Boudreaux."

Mike whistled softly. "The lady keeps high company."

"Yeah." Roarke rubbed his jaw, irritated by a nagging feeling that felt too much like jealousy for comfort. "It's also interesting that, during his press conference, Boudreaux didn't mention anything about his fiancée, who just happens to be a deputy prosecutor, being missing."

"Perhaps he doesn't know."

"He's got to know that the fibbie was killed in a hotel room she reserved for some unknown reason."

"The police aren't giving out her name," Mike reminded his brother.

"Yeah, but we both know NOPD leaks like a rusty sieve. I tell you, whatever's going on, I have the feeling Boudreaux's involved."

"You think *he* shot her?" Although Mike remained outwardly relaxed, Roarke knew his older brother well enough to recognize the professional interest. He suddenly reminded him of Elvis, their old German bluetick hound, at point. Once a cop, always a cop, he figured.

"I'm not saying that." Personally, Roarke felt such actions would be too direct for the politician.

"But it's more than the fact that you're still harboring a grudge from the time we had to beat the guy up for jumping Shayne on the basketball court back in junior high," Mike guessed.

Despite the seriousness of the situation, Roarke smiled at the memory. "It's a helluva lot more than that. I just felt, watching him, that he knows a lot more than he's saying. Which wouldn't be that surprising, given the fact that he doesn't want to blow the case. But he's mixed up in this, Mike. Right up to the knot in his pretty silk necktie."

"I'll run a discreet background check on Boudreaux. See what he's up to these days. Who he might be hanging out with."

"Thanks. I appreciate that." Enjoying the unqualified fraternal support, Roarke wondered why it had been so long since he'd been home.

"No problem." Mike rubbed his chin and chose his words carefully. "By the way, I also looked into your mystery woman."

"Daria?" Roarke wondered why that should irritate him. It was, after all, a smart and prudent thing to do. "You checked up on her?"

"I didn't want to find you with a bullet in the back of the head," Mike said mildly. "But if anyone's going to shoot you, it isn't going to be her. The lady's so clean she squeaks."

Roarke knew he was in deep, deep trouble when relief flooded over him. He shouldn't care. He didn't want to care, dammit. But he did.

"I'm glad to hear that."

Mike grinned, not fooled at all by his brother's casual tone. "Yeah, I just bet you are."

They left the zoo together and took Mike's car to Daria's Irish Channel house. The Victorian cottage was located in a working-class section that was undergoing regentrification. Mike was all too familiar with it, having spent more than a few nights beneath the cute little blue fishscale roof.

"Funny thing, coincidence," he murmured as he pulled into the driveway.

Roarke glanced over at him. "I assume there's a point to that statement?"

"This used to be Désirée's house. Your mystery lady must have bought it from her when she married Roman Falconer and moved to the French Quarter."

Roarke thought he detected a note of regret in Mike's voice. "Having regrets about letting the lovely newslady get away?"

"Naw. It never would have worked. After Désirée and I broke up, I went out with a producer at the station for a few months. She'd watched Désirée and me during the months we were together and told me she'd decided our problem was we both insisted on being right. All of the time."

Roarke laughed at the pithy, all-too-true analysis. "Sounds like one smart lady. So, what happened to her?"

Mike shrugged. "She got offered a job at the network. It's hard for a working stiff to compete with the razzle-dazzle of the big city."

Roarke knew he was prejudiced, but he still couldn't imagine any woman choosing a career over his brother. Granted, *he* would undoubtedly make a lousy husband. And Shayne was probably even worse. But if there was ever a man who was husband material, it was Michael O'Malley.

"You must not have tried very hard to keep her."

"That's much the same thing she said when we said our goodbyes at the airport." A wry grin twitched Mike's lips. "I guess it was pretty much the truth. I liked Karyn a lot. And we got along great, but it was more like she was my sister. Or a favorite cousin. I didn't ever have that drowning feeling when I was with her."

He glanced over at Roarke, his expression revealing that he wasn't entirely comfortable talking about these failed relationships, even with his brother. "Know what I mean?"

"All too well," Roarke muttered as he opened the car door.

The interior of the cozy little home was a monument to romanticism. Violets bloomed on cream walls, needlepoint carpets covered pine plank floors that had been polished to a bright shine. It would have been lovely—if someone hadn't recently trashed it.

"Damn," Mike muttered.

Roarke's curse was riper and a great deal harsher as he stood in the doorway, staring at the destruction. Needlepoint pictures had been ripped from the walls, the frames broken by whoever had been intent on searching behind their paper backings. The flowered upholstery on the sofa had been slashed, the foam material from the cushions scattered over the floor like unmelted snow. Books had been torn apart, pages ripped from their bindings. This was no ordinary vandalism.

"What were they looking for?" he wondered out loud.

"I wonder if they found it," Mike countered. "Or if the lady still has it in her possession."

"I searched her purse. There wasn't anything in there that anyone would trash a place looking for."

"Well, so far, they've killed a federal attorney, shot a deputy prosecutor and trashed her house. Whoever these guys are, they're not going to stop until they get what they're looking for. And shut the lady up."

Roarke refused to even consider that possibility. "We're just going to have to get to them first."

"Good idea." Mike's dry tone didn't quite conceal the amusement he felt at the realization that his world-roving, playboy brother was hooked. If the situation wasn't so deadly, it would be downright humorous. "Meanwhile, let's just get the lady's clothes and get out of here."

They went into the bedroom, where more flowers—pink rosebuds this time—covered the walls. The dresser had been overturned and her clothing scattered over the floor. Roarke picked up a pair of skimpy black silk-and-lace panties that had been slashed by an unseen knife for no other reason than to give the vandal some sick, erotic pleasure.

Fury rose like bile in his throat at the idea of some cretin touching Daria's frothy underwear. "I'll kill the guy for this alone."

His tone was soft and dangerous. Mike, who'd been checking out the adjoining bathroom, returned and studied him grimly. "You realize, of course, when it gets personal is when it gets dangerous."

Roarke knew that only too well. He did, after all, have the scars—physical and emotional—to remind him of that little lesson. "Yeah. I know. But unfortunately, it doesn't change things."

"No." Mike sighed, dragged his fingers through his hair and gave him the same worried look Roarke remembered receiving after getting busted for shoplifting. "I don't know whether to congratulate you or ask Mom to say a novena for her middle son."

Roarke laughed at that, which eased the pressure that had been building inside him. "Let's get the stuff and get out of here. I'm pretty sure Daria's safe so long as she stays where she is, but—"

"You're afraid she won't stay put."

"Things are starting to come back to her," Roarke said. "I'm afraid she'll remember something she thinks is important and go tearing out and get herself shot again."

Mike gave the room another longer perusal. "Want to call this vandalism in?"

"I don't think so. It's obvious the bad guys are keeping a low profile. And since they just happen to be cops, it'd probably behoove us to do the same."

"Great minds," Mike murmured, suggesting they were on the same track. "Meanwhile, while you pack, I think I'll have a little chat with the neighbors. See if they noticed anything."

Roarke picked up an ivory froth of a nightgown and felt a renewed surge of anger as he viewed the jagged slashes, obviously made with a knife, across the front of the lacy bodice. "Good idea."

Five minutes later they met on the sidewalk again.

How to validate your
Editor's FREE GIFT "Thank You"

1. Peel off gift seal from front cover. Place it in space provided at right. This automatically entitles you to receive four free books and a lovely simulated cultured pearl necklace.

2. Send back this card and you'll get brand-new Harlequin Temptation® novels. These books have a cover price of $3.50 each, but they are yours to keep absolutely free.

3. There's no catch. You're under no obligation to buy anything. We charge nothing—ZERO—for your first shipment. And you don't have to make any minimum number of purchases—not even one!

4. The fact is thousands of readers enjoy receiving books by mail from the Harlequin Reader Service®. They like the convenience of home delivery...they like getting the best new novels BEFORE they're available in stores... and they love our discount prices!

5. We hope that after receiving your free books you'll want to remain a subscriber. But the choice is yours— to continue or cancel, any time at all! So why not take us up on our invitation, with no risk of any kind. You'll be glad you did!

6. Don't forget to detach your FREE BOOKMARK. And remember...just for validating your Editor's Free Gift Offer we'll send you FIVE MORE gifts, *ABSOLUTELY FREE!*

GET A FREE NECKLACE...

This lovely necklace will add glamour to your most elegant outfit! Its cobra-link chain is a generous 18" long, and its lustrous simulated cultured pearl is mounted in an attractive pendant! Best of all, it's absolutely free, just for accepting our no-risk offer!

The Editor's "Thank You" Free Gifts Include:

- Four BRAND-NEW romance novels!
- A lovely simulated cultured pearl necklace!

PLACE FREE GIFT SEAL HERE

YES! I have placed my Editor's "Thank You" seal in the space provided above. Please send me 4 free books and a lovely simulated pearl necklace. I understand I am under no obligation to purchase any books, as explained on the back and on the opposite page.

142 CIH A7ZP (U-H-T-06/97)

Name

Address   Apt.

City

State   Zip

Thank You!

BUSINESS REPLY MAIL
FIRST-CLASS MAIL   PERMIT NO. 717   BUFFALO, NY

POSTAGE WILL BE PAID BY ADDRESSEE

HARLEQUIN READER SERVICE
3010 WALDEN AVE
PO BOX 1867
BUFFALO NY 14240-9952

NO POSTAGE
NECESSARY
IF MAILED
IN THE
UNITED STATES

"None of the neighbors are home," Mike said. "They probably work. I've got a meeting to go to, but since I doubt if our guys did this in the daylight, it'd probably be better just to come back tonight and see what I can find out."

"You don't have to do that. Surely you've got cases—"

"None as important as this one." When Roarke looked inclined to argue, Mike held up a broad hand. "Hey, Mom's been after me to provide her with grandchildren. The way I figure it, if I can get either you or Shayne married off, she'll get off my back."

"If you're counting on me to get married, you're going to have a very long wait," Roarke warned. He threw the overnight case into the back seat. "You've always been the feet-on-the-ground O'Malley brother. Why don't *you* get hitched?"

"Because marriage is a commitment that a guy hopefully only makes once in a lifetime. And even in this city renowned for gorgeous women, it's not that easy finding the right one—the one I can picture myself growing old with."

"I think the trick is not to get old in the first place."

"Well, if that's your plan," Mike drawled as he unlocked the driver's door, "from the looks of this latest mess you've gotten yourself involved in, you're going about it in the right way."

Since Roarke reluctantly decided Mike had a point, he didn't bother to argue.

They drove back to where Roarke had left his car in the Audubon Park lot. It wasn't until he was driving back down Saint Charles toward the safe house that he realized he was being tailed.

"Damn." He cast a look in the rearview mirror, then

cut into the other lane. The unmarked white police sedan followed. Not wanting to lead whoever it was to Daria, he turned in the opposite direction, away from the safe house, and drove past Loyola University, north toward Interstate 90. Unsurprisingly, the white car followed.

Roarke considered his options. He could spend the day driving all over the city, but outrunning cops wasn't all that easy. Especially when you were driving a Porsche 911 that stood out like a sore thumb and you couldn't tell the bad guys from the good guys.

As he approached Tulane Stadium, he saw cars in the parking lot and realized that although football season was over, something was going on. Deciding that they couldn't kill him in front of witnesses, Roarke pulled into the lot, drove as close as he could to the stadium and cut the engine.

The cops pulled up behind him, which he'd expected. What he hadn't expected was the marked police car that came from nowhere to park in front of him, effectively cutting off any escape. Realizing that he'd just made a tactical error, Roarke cursed and rolled down his window.

The two cops from the car behind his could have come from Central Casting. One was short and skinny with a pointed face that reminded Roarke of a weasel. The other was about six foot two, and obviously enjoyed his po'boys, beans and rice. The material of his blue shirt strained across his broad belly, threatening to pop buttons, and as he neared, Roarke noticed Tabasco-sauce stains. Both men were wearing mirrored sunglasses that prevented him from seeing their eyes.

He had no doubt he could take them both. But not the other two, who had remained in their car. Waiting.

He turned the key to roll down the window. When the ignition caught, the skinny cop's hand went immediately to the holster clipped to the side of his slacks.

"What's wrong, officers?" He gave them the same harmless, I-want-to-be-your-friend smile he'd given the Serbian guards manning the roadblock on the road leading into Herzegovina. "If I was speeding—"

"Can the small talk and get out of the car." The large cop's voice reminded Roarke of the growl of a bear just waking up after hibernation.

Extremely thankful that he'd told Mike the address of the safe house, just in case he ran into trouble, Roarke did as instructed.

"I don't suppose you'd like to see my license."

"We heard you were a clever man." The little cop smirked. "Are you clever enough to pass on a message to your girlfriend?"

"I don't have any idea who you're referring to. Officer." Roarke tacked on the last word slowly and deliberately, his voice thick with scorn. He also refrained, with effort, from punching the bastard right in the mouth.

The two cops exchanged a look. "Guess he isn't so smart, after all," the big one said to the skinny one.

"Your mama should have taught you to use better manners when talking to the po-leece," the cop said as he grabbed Roarke's arms and with surprising strength for such a beanpole, jerked them behind Roarke's back in a way that strained his shoulder joints. "Now, the officer is going to ask you a few questions. And you're going to answer real polite-like. Got that?"

"And the mayor wonders why the police don't get any respect," Roarke drawled.

The sarcastic remark instantly earned him a huge fist in the midsection. Biting his lip to keep from moaning, Roarke reminded himself that he'd survived worse. Much, much worse.

"Where's the woman?"

"I told you—"

The huge fists came crashing down on his head. Roarke felt the asphalt beneath his feet tilt. When he tried to jerk away, he got a bony knee jabbed into his back, reminding him again that he was outnumbered.

"We're not going to hurt her. She stole something of ours. As soon as she gives it back, everything will be all right."

"Even if I knew who or what you were talking about, which I don't," Roarke lied without a qualm, "I have a personal rule against making deals with dirty cops."

The answering blow brought a monstrous bolt of pain to his rib cage.

"You can spare yourself all this. Just give her to us. She can't mean that much to you. No woman's worth dying for."

There had been a time after the car bombing, when he'd been furious at Natasha for having set him up, at the mobsters who'd rigged the bomb, and most of all, furious with himself for being such a chump, that Roarke might have agreed.

But his relationship with Natasha had been about sex. And although he didn't have the foggiest idea what was happening between him and Daria, he suspected that like it or not, they had already moved beyond that.

It wasn't that Roarke was afraid of death; he'd faced it down and won on numerous occasions in his life. He just damn well didn't want to die right now. But neither would he give them Daria.

He was held helpless as the Neanderthal cop hammered at him with huge, mallet-like fists.

"Dammit, just tell us where she is!"

A grunt escaped from between Roarke's clenched teeth. He shook his head, experiencing a blinding shaft of pain behind his eyes.

"You know we'll find her. And what's happening to you now will seem like a picnic," the voice rasped in his ear. "There are several people who'll enjoy watching the ice-maiden bitch crack."

Ice maiden? If he hadn't been concentrating on not throwing up all over his shoes, Roarke would have laughed at that description.

"You see my partner has this unfortunate little quirk. He likes to inflict pain," the man standing behind him said. "Especially on women. And although her actions the other night suggest that she'll put up a fight, that will only add to the fun."

The thought of either of these men putting so much as a finger on Daria caused Roarke to explode with fury. Beyond caring that his enraged counterattack could only prove futile, he jerked free and shot an incautious fist toward his attacker, connecting with the wide bridge of his nose.

"Dammit!" the giant roared.

The other cop didn't say anything. But the gun crashing down on the back of Roarke's skull spoke volumes. It also brought stars. Roarke reached out blindly, grabbing at the car for support, refusing to allow his body to crumple to the ground.

The big cop, proving that it wasn't just fat bulging beneath that stained shirt, literally picked Roarke up off his feet and threw him to the ground. Although he tried to roll out of harm's way, a well-placed kick crunched heavily into his rib cage and he lay on his back, his mouth open and his eyes shut, gasping for breath like a grounded carp.

He felt cold metal against his temple and realized with a detached pragmatism that this time he was probably going to die. He also found it interesting that his last thoughts were going to be of Daria. She was so lovely. So warm. And soft.

Roarke thought about the perfumed scent of her hair, her silky skin, her sweet, sweet taste, the way she'd trembled in his arms, and he decided that his last regret would be not having made love to Daria Shea when he'd had the chance.

So lost was he in his mental escape, Roarke failed to notice the woman approaching.

"What the hell are you men doing?" she demanded in a voice loud enough to awaken the dead in Saint Louis cemetery No. 1.

Roarke opened one eye and saw a woman in her mid-sixties moving toward them like a tall ship at full sail, a scowl like a Gulf Coast squall on her wide dark face.

"Police," the skinny cop said, flashing a badge. When he saw Roarke trying to focus on it, he immediately closed the vinyl folder and jammed it back into his pocket. The other police car slowly slid away, Roarke noticed with interest. And relief.

"You think I don't know that?" The woman displayed not an ounce of trepidation. Nor respect. "You're the kinda police who give the city a bad name." She looked down at Roarke. "What did you do to get that pretty face all bashed in?"

"Ran a stop sign?"

She shook her head in ill-concealed disgust. "Attitude like that can get you beat up on general principle." She looked back at the cops. "I'm Hattie Long." A smile spread across her face as she watched recognition dawn on the two cops' faces. "That's right. Head of the joint police/citizens' council on police reform. We're having ourselves a little rally here and the police chief himself just finished talking to the crowd. In fact, if you two officers want to wait just a sec, I'll go get him and—"

The skinny cop's answer was harsh, rude and anatomically impossible. It also made her laugh, a bold rich laugh that reminded Roarke of friendly thunder moving over the bayou.

Hattie watched with satisfaction as the cops climbed back into the unmarked car and drove away. "Guess that took care of them," she said, looking down at Roarke.

He managed, with effort, to ignore his roiling stomach and sit up. "I don't know how to thank you."

"No thanks necessary. Us good folks got to stick together. That's what the rally's all about." She jerked her head toward the stadium from where, now that he concentrated on it and his heart was no longer pounding in his ears, Roarke could hear cheering.

"How did you know I wasn't one of the bad guys?"

"Honey, you might be. In fact, I'll bet there's a lot of women who can attest that you can be *real* bad. But I know *you* from the television. And I know *them* from the streets."

"I owe you."

"Maybe you can do a report about the commission. Get some more people to join us."

"You've got it. As soon as I look presentable enough to go on the air without frightening little children."

She folded her arms across her abundant breasts. "Seems to me if you're going to go on the air with a story about police brutality, you look just about right."

"Good point." Needlelike bursts of pain shot through Roarke's head as he struggled to his feet, causing a dizzy, spinning nausea in his stomach. "You ever think of going into broadcast news?"

"And give up my job?"

He leaned against the Porsche. "What do you do?" He wasn't really in the mood for small talk, but felt obligated to her for having saved his life.

Her next words reminded Roarke of the dangers of stereotyping. "I'm a criminal-law professor at Loyola." She laughed at the surprise on his face. "Yeah, everyone reacts that way."

"I'm sorry. I don't usually—"

"Don't worry about it, handsome. It's one of my small pleasures in life."

Her good humor was contagious. Roarke found himself smiling back.

Her next words proved even more surprising. "Want me to call your brother?"

"You know Mike?"

Stupid question. Everyone in the city probably knew his big brother. Especially after all the press he'd gotten when he'd apprehended the serial rapist who'd been terrorizing the city. He'd shot the guy in Désirée's house, Roarke remembered belatedly, wondering if Daria knew of her home's history. For such a pretty little house, it had definitely been the scene of a surprising amount of violence.

"He just happens to be cochair of the committee." She linked their arms, effectively steadying him. "He was scheduled to speak after the mayor."

"Small world," Roarke muttered.

"Ain't it just," Dr. Hattie Long said with a chuckle.

8

HATTIE SENT WORD for Mike to meet them in the stadium office.

"Lord Almighty." He dragged his hand down his face and shook his head. "You look like you've been run over by a parade float."

"I feel like it was the entire damn parade."

"Do you know who beat you up?"

"No. But it'd be my educated guess that it wasn't a welcoming committee."

Mike looked thoughtful. "If they were actually going to kill you—"

"They weren't. They just wanted me to give them Daria."

"Which, of course, you refused to do."

"Of course." The eye that wasn't rapidly swelling shut gave Michael a challenging look.

"Good for you." Mike gave him another longer, more critical look. "We need to get you to the hospital."

"Naw. I'll be fine. Really," he insisted, watching the dubious expression move across his brother's face. A face that resembled the one he looked at each morning in the mirror while shaving, but was more harshly hewn. "Nothing's broken. I'm just going to be sore for a few days. They were cops, Mike. If I go to the hospital, they'll find me. And believe me, that isn't something I'm real eager to have happen."

Mike exhaled a frustrated breath, but his expression revealed he'd expected no other answer. "You and Daria need to get out of the city for a few days. Let her regain her memory. Then, at least we'll know who the bad guys are. And why they're after her. In the meantime, I'll E-mail you some employment records. You can see if you recognize any of the cops."

Roarke lifted a brow. "Isn't it against the law to break into police-department computer files?"

"It's against the law for cops to go beating up law-abiding civilians," Mike countered. "And that's just for starters. If the trail leads from that body in the Whitfield Palace to the cop shop, this city's going to blow sky-high."

"You've had dirty cops before."

"True. Even some killers. But blowing away federal attorneys is beyond the pale. Even for New Orleans." He rubbed his square jaw again. "They'll probably be watching for me. Let me get someone else to drive you back to the house."

Even more worried about Daria than he'd been earlier, Roarke agreed. Ten minutes later, a huge, bald African-American wearing a white leather trench coat arrived at the stadium office.

"Roarke, this is Sugar. Sugar, my famous TV-star brother, Roarke O'Malley."

"Sugar?"

The giant's glower could have cut the steel girders on the Huey P. Long Bridge. "You got a problem with my name?"

Having already had his face used as a punching

bag, Roarke was in no mood to repeat the experience. "Not at all."

"Didn't think so." Sugar glanced over at Mike, who was trying his best to hold back a grin and failing badly. "Baby brother catches on real fast."

"He always was a quick study."

"Too bad he never learned not to stick his nose where it don't belong."

"We all have flaws," Mike reminded him. "Except you, of course."

"Oh, I got me a flaw, all right," Sugar grumbled. "Whatever it was that made me decide to leave WSLU and come work for you."

"If you'd rather go back to spending your days filming new lion cubs born at the zoo, you're free to leave."

Sugar flashed a long black middle finger, then turned and walked back out the door, ducking to avoid hitting his head on the frame.

Roarke watched him leave, then glanced over at his brother. "I take it I'm supposed to follow him?"

"That'd be my suggestion. Unless you want to walk home. Sugar's not one for standing around shooting the breeze. But what he lacks in conversational skills, he definitely makes up in loyalty."

"And size," Roarke murmured.

"Doesn't hurt when the bad guys are after you."

"Especially when they're packing police pistols." Roarke gave his brother a quick salute. "Thanks again." He turned to his rescuer. "I'll tape the initial stuff today, before the bruises fade. Then, when I break this other story I'm working on, I'll work on the angle of cops beating up civilians."

Hattie Long nodded her pewter-gray head. "I'd appreciate that."

"Hey, I owe you. Big time." He wiped his mouth to make certain it wasn't still bleeding, and kissed her cheek. Then followed Sugar out to a red van with Tricou's Cajun Fish Market painted on the side in green letters. The interior of the van smelled of boiled crayfish.

Mike was definitely right about Sugar's not being a dazzling conversationalist. A wave of his huge arm told Roarke he was expected to lie down in the back of the van, which wasn't that much of a sacrifice, since his head had begun to spin again and he decided he would rather die on the spot than show weakness by fainting in front of this man. They stopped at the Porsche and Sugar retrieved his and Daria's luggage.

"Your friends be waiting for you," Sugar said as they drove out of the stadium parking lot.

Roarke wasn't surprised. "How many?"

"A squad car. And an unmarked." Sugar glanced in the rearview mirror. "They not moving. Looks like we ditched them."

Roarke suspected the Shaft street vernacular was put-on, but wasn't about to challenge Sugar on it. "You look familiar," he said instead.

"You know what they say about us all looking alike."

"Cute," Roarke muttered. He wasn't feeling up to playing Twenty Questions. But it had been nagging at him since Sugar had first strolled in the door.

Sugar's only response was a shrug of his massive shoulders.

It was the shoulders that rang the bell. Roarke knew

he'd seen them before, but looking even wider in football pads.

"You played defensive line for Louisiana State," he remembered suddenly.

There was no answer from the front seat.

"I played for Vanderbilt. You beat us four years in a row."

"Everybody beat Vanderbilt," Sugar drawled. "And yeah, I remember whupping your skinny ass. You thought you wanted to be a running back. But you were a step slow."

"More than a step," Roarke muttered, recalling his inglorious collegiate-sports career. "You broke my collarbone."

"You were headed toward the goal line. Couldn't let you score."

He had, Roarke admitted, a point. "Didn't I read you went into pro wrestling?"

"How you expect me to know what you read?" Sugar countered.

Roarke decided he'd just stumbled onto a touchy area and didn't respond. But he welcomed the puzzle since it took his mind off the pain. The giant driving the fish van, the former linebacker who was now working for his brother, had done a stint in the World Federation Wrestling Association, Roarke recalled. Billed as The Dark Avenger, Sugar had been an immediate hit with the audiences. According to rumors on the sports pages, his career had been cut short when he couldn't get it through his head that he was supposed to be *pretending* to break his opponents in two.

Deciding he couldn't be in better hands, given the circumstances, Roarke closed his eyes and, utilizing visualization techniques he'd learned after getting shot by a sniper in Sarajevo in the early days of the war, he allowed his mind to drift to more pleasant topics.

He envisioned lying with Daria in front of a roaring fire, in a chalet somewhere in the French Alps. Balloon glasses of brandy were on a table nearby; their discarded clothes made a path from the door to the fur rug. He'd just lowered his head to take the taut rosy peak of one of her breasts between his lips when a deep voice shattered the erotic fantasy.

"I need the gate code." Sugar's impatient tone suggested this was not the first time he'd asked.

"Right." Roarke dragged himself from the chalet back to reality. The first sequence of numbers proved wrong.

"Don't take all night," Sugar said. "I got me a stakeout to get to over in Iberville."

"Give me a minute."

The second try was no more successful. Sugar's succinct curse implied that Roarke's memory was as bad as his skill on the gridiron.

"Maybe if I just pushed the buttons," Roarke suggested. "Thinking about it only makes it worse."

Although his expression revealed that he was less than enthusiastic about this approach, Sugar moved over into the passenger seat, and Roarke came forward and took his.

Roarke closed his eyes. Cleared his mind. Then opened his eyes and tried again. Fortunately, his fingers recalled what his mind had forgotten and this time the gate slid obediently open, allowing Roarke to drive through. He used the same technique successfully on the garage door.

"I'll tell your brother you got home safely," Sugar

said. His expression remained as inscrutable as the Sphinx, but Roarke thought he caught a fleeting glimpse of, if not warmth, at least respect when the bald giant mentioned his brother. "You take care, now."

"I will." Roarke held out his hand and watched it disappear into Sugar's massive dark one. "And thanks a lot. You may well have saved my life."

"That's my job," Sugar drawled. "Instead of beating white guy's asses, these days I save 'em." The thought seemed to give him immense amusement and he was still chuckling as he backed out of the garage, leaving Roarke to face Daria.

"Oh, my God!" Daria's hand flew to her mouth as she viewed Roarke. "What on earth happened?"

"If you think I look bad, you should see the other guys." Roarke vowed that before this was over, he was going to even the score with those thugs. He put the cases down beside the door.

"Were they waiting at my house?"

"They must have been." Roarke was furious at himself for not having noticed them lurking somewhere nearby when he and Mike had first arrived. "I'm afraid I've got bad news."

He thought of the pretty little lace pillows that had been ripped apart on the bed, the needlework ripped from its frames, the broken perfume bottles. And, worst of all, the torn lingerie. "They trashed your place pretty badly."

"I don't care about that." She brushed his news away with a flick of her wrist. "They're just things." She reached up and placed a hand against his cheek, which was already turning a darker purple than her own bruised one. "Those men who beat you up were after me, weren't they?"

Roarke knew better than to lie. "Yeah. But I wouldn't have let them get you, Daria."

"I know."

Roarke liked her touching him. He also liked the way she looked. The bruise on her face was already fading and she'd raided the closets and changed into a pair of men's boxer shorts, socks and a T-shirt that, although oversize, nevertheless clung to her body in all the right places.

"I wonder what they were looking for," she murmured.

"I was hoping you could tell me. They mentioned something about your having something that belonged to them. Obviously, since they came after me, trying to get to you, they didn't find whatever it is in the house."

Although he hadn't liked thinking it, on the way back to the house he'd been forced to consider that she had been lying all along. But for what purpose?

"I feel so guilty about this." Daria had spent the entire time he'd been gone trying to think of something that would explain why someone would be willing to kill her and had come up blank. "You said you went through my purse...?"

"I didn't find anything worth killing anyone for."

"Maybe whoever it was who shot me and beat you up is wrong. Maybe I don't have what they're looking for. Maybe I never did."

"There's always that chance." He'd thought of the same thing himself. Then he remembered how she'd been hanging on to that purse so tightly when she'd left the hotel.

Frustrated, Daria turned her attention to the more immediate problem. "We need to get you to bed."

He smiled at that. Slowly, infuriatingly. "Although that's the best offer I've heard all day, sweetheart, I think I'd better pass. I'm not certain I'd be capable of my usual stunning performance right now."

Daria had no doubt that the words, edged with sarcasm, were intended to throw cold water on the flames that had blazed between them before he'd left the house to meet his brother. Refusing to let him see how badly they stung, she threw a cool smile right back at him.

"I love a man who knows his limitations."

Her dry tone was at odds with the color in her cheeks, but Roarke gave her points for trying.

"There are times when knowing the difference between desire and ability can keep you alive. Besides," he added, "taking you to bed would probably be the worst mistake I've ever made. And believe me, baby, I've made some doozies."

Although she'd insisted she was not going to make love with him, Roarke's rejection hurt.

"Don't you want me?"

His answer was a harsh laugh. "What the hell do you think?"

"I don't know," she admitted. "As confused as I am about everything—who I am, how I got into this mess, why anyone would want to kill me—I'm even more confused about whatever it is that's happening between you and me."

"Nothing's happening but sexual chemistry. Pure and simple. Which is why, although it's probably going to be the hardest thing I've ever done, I'm going to resist doing what I've wanted to do ever since you first kissed me."

A humdinger of a kiss, she reminded herself again. "Then you *do* want me?"

This time his rough laugh was entirely without humor. "Why don't you just ask me if I want to breathe? Hell, yes, I want you. More than I can remember wanting any woman in my life. But the timing's all wrong."

He had a point. But still...

"What about when it's over?" she asked, feeling more vulnerable than she'd felt when she'd awakened in that hospital and not known who she was.

Roarke swore. "In case it's slipped your mind, you're engaged."

"Engagements have been broken."

"True. And personally, if you want my opinion, I think you're better off without James Boudreaux. He's a twenty-four-karat phony who's so wrapped up in himself and his ambition, that he'd be too blind to realize what a jewel he was getting when he married you."

He'd called her a jewel! Daria felt as if she were beaming from the inside out.

Roarke watched the pleasure light up her face and groaned inwardly when he realized that by trying to discourage her, he'd gotten himself—and her—in deeper. He was going to do his damnedest to keep her alive, but he also feared there was no way to keep her from getting hurt before all this was over.

"You deserve more than Boudreaux's willing to give you," he said. "And a helluva lot more than I can give you."

"And now you're assuming you know what I want? What I need?"

He dragged his hand through his hair. "Dammit, there's things you don't know about me."

"Then tell me."

He sighed heavily, and felt the pain in his bruised ribs. "You were definitely born to the law, sweetheart. Because I feel as if I'm undergoing a cross-examination. You remind me a lot of Michael."

Roarke thought about the similarities between the brother he'd always loved and a woman he was beginning to care too much about. "In fact, the two of you would probably make a perfect match. Maybe when all this is over and the bad guys are locked away behind bars, you and Mike can pull off a Technicolor happy ending."

"As nice as your brother seemed, I don't want him. I want you." Daria was sure she'd never begged for a man in her life. She couldn't believe she was actually willing to beg for Roarke. "Not now, while you're injured. But I've never felt this way about another man."

"How do you know?" he retorted, growing more frustrated as the conversation continued. "You've lost your memory."

"I'd know that." She tilted her chin in an argumentative way that made him want to kiss her silly. "I also know that at the end of our lives it's not necessarily what we've *done* that we regret. But what we haven't done."

Mindless of the dried blood staining the front of his sweater, she gently touched his chest. "I don't want to regret not making love to you."

He caught her hand. "That's the definitive word, baby. *Love.* You should hold out for a man capable of loving you the way you deserve to be loved."

"And that's not you."

"No." The ability to love had been blown away in that explosion. "And now that we've got that settled, I have to tape a stand-up for a friend."

"You can do that later."

"I need to do it now. Hattie may have saved my life by coming along when she did. I owe her this."

The thought that he could have been killed on her account was too horrendous to contemplate. Daria pressed her hand against his chest again, noticing that even that light touch caused him to suck in a pained breath.

"Do you need help?"

What he needed, dammit, was her. "With what?"

"Your stand-up. If you need someone to hold the camera..."

"Naw." He shrugged, then flinched. "I can handle it. I only want to document the damage those guys did while I still look like roadkill. Then I'll get to the story later."

Realizing that she may just have met an individual every bit as stubborn as herself, Daria knew there was no point in arguing. Roarke was going to do exactly what he wanted to do, and nothing she could say would change that.

"Why don't I get you a drink? And some of those pain pills you promised me last night?"

"I'll skip the pills." He doubted the rogue cops could find this place but he didn't want to fog his mind, just in case he and Daria had to make a quick getaway. "But I sure wouldn't turn down a drink."

"I'll get it right away." Daria was pleased to have the chance to take care of him for a change. "I saw some decanters in the library. Would Scotch be okay? Or perhaps brandy?"

"Scotch'll be fine."

"I'll go get it. And meet you upstairs."

"Sounds great." He watched the sway of Daria's slender hips as she left the room, and although he knew it was masochistic even allowing his mind to wander off in that direction, Roarke envisioned sharing a hot steamy shower with her.

That alone would be worth getting beaten up.

It only took a few minutes to set up the minicam and tape the opening sequence. Then, deciding a long hot shower might be just what the doctor ordered, he headed upstairs.

Daria was waiting for him in the tiled bathroom. She had run him a bath and the room was filled with fragrant steam.

"You put in bubble bath?"

She appeared unmoved by the disapproval in his tone. "It's called aromatherapy. It's supposed to be relaxing."

"I'm going to smell like a girl," he complained as the scent of jasmine and gardenia surrounded him in a fragrant cloud.

"Don't worry, Roarke." She reached up and unbuttoned the three buttons at the throat of his sweater. "No one could ever mistake you for a woman." She caught hold of the sweater's hem and, with his help, pulled it over his head. "Oh, my God!"

Her expression as she took in the sight of his bare chest was one of horror.

"It's not that bad," he said again. "Besides, I'll heal. I always do."

Daria couldn't prevent her eyes filling with moisture. "This is all my fault. If I hadn't come up to you in the Blue Bayou, if I hadn't dragged you into my problems—"

"I would have missed a helluva story." He picked up the glass she'd put on the marble counter and took a long swallow, willing the Scotch to soothe his aching body. "I'm a grown man, Daria. Capable of making my own choices."

"But if you'd known that leaving that lounge with me would have gotten you so brutally beaten up—"

"I would have gone along with you in a heartbeat."

His answer was so quick, so sure, Daria had no choice but to believe him. "Why?" she whispered.

It was a question he'd been asking himself from the beginning. The answer had struck like a lightning bolt from a clear blue summer sky while he'd been lying in the back of Sugar's van.

"Because I didn't have a choice."

"Everyone has choices." As soon as she'd said the words, Daria realized they were what she always said when some defense attorney tried to explain that a defendant's less-than-ideal upbringing had left him or her devoid of opportunity or choice.

"I used to think that." His cracked lip pulled into a faint, self-mocking smile as he recalled how he'd once prided himself on his ability to select his own path in life. "I don't anymore."

She looked inclined to argue. Then, when he began to unfasten the metal button on his jeans, apparently changed her mind.

"I guess I'll let you take your bath," she murmured.

"You can always stick around if you want." Another button followed. "We can talk about the case. See if we can jog your memory a bit."

Daria knew it was a test. One she was destined to

fail. Because there was no way she could stay in this warm, steamy room with a naked Roarke O'Malley and think about anything but the dizzying way he made her feel.

"Perhaps later."

She flashed him another of those cool false smiles he figured she pulled out to use on the opposing counsel in court. Then she left the room, closing the door behind her.

Sighing, and letting his shoulders slump with pain for the first time since he'd arrived back at the house, Roarke finished undressing then lowered himself into the warm water, sipped his Scotch and tried to focus on what, exactly, Daria could have done to make James Boudreaux want to kill her.

He was lost in thought, wondering if any politician would actually kill if someone discovered that he'd been taking illegal campaign contributions, when there was a knock on the door.

"May I come in?"

He hesitated, then decided that if she didn't mind seeing him naked, it didn't bother him. "Sure."

"I've been thinking." She focused her attention on his face.

"About the case?"

"No." Her hands were behind her back; the mirror revealed her nervousness by the way she was twisting them together. "About what you said. You know, about love and sex." Her voice was strong, but watching her carefully, Roarke saw the slight tremor of her all-too-kissable bottom lip.

"And?"

"And you're probably right about our attraction being due to our situation. Danger is undoubtedly a powerful aphrodisiac."

"You've got that right."

"So, we'll keep it physical. Enjoy each other while we can. And then when it's over, and, as you said, the bad guys are behind bars, we'll each move on with our lives."

Roarke arched an eyebrow, surprised by how even that faint movement pained. "You'd be willing to settle for that?"

"Yes." Daria had no idea if that was the truth or not. But she did know it was the only possible answer under the circumstances.

The eye that wasn't practically swollen shut narrowed. "Let me get this straight. You think you're capable of having hot steamy sex with me—for however many days and nights it takes to solve these murders—then blithely shaking hands, putting on a lacy white wedding dress and walking down the aisle with your fiancé?"

"I'm not sure about marrying James...." It was more than the fact she couldn't remember being engaged to him. There was some other reason, hovering on the very edges of her consciousness.

"Aha!" he said, as if finding the flaw in her argument.

Daria ignored his triumphant tone. "And, if we're going to be having all this hot steamy sex, I think I'd prefer a goodbye kiss rather than a handshake.

"But yes, that's what I'm saying. I'm capable of making my own decisions. And if I want to have an affair with you, and you want to have sex with me, since we're both adults, it doesn't seem like there's anything to stop us."

She made it sound so simple. Too simple. Roarke knew there was a trap somewhere; he just couldn't concentrate on searching it out when his body ached as if it had been used for a punching bag. Which it had been.

"You have to admit, it's the perfect solution." She took a burgundy washcloth down from the antique gold ring and knelt beside the tub. Roarke's pain was forgotten as he watched her deliberate, almost-seductive movements.

She dipped the washcloth in the water, then gently washed away the dried blood on his face with a tenderness he'd only ever received from his mother. He'd been eight years old, covered with chicken pox that itched like the devil. Years later, he could still remember the soothing touch of Mary O'Malley's fingers as they'd smoothed the pink calamine lotion over those red bumps.

Of course his mother's touch, as wonderful as it had been, had not excited him in the same way Daria's did as she trailed the cloth down his throat and over his chest.

"It's an attractive solution," he admitted. "I'm not certain it's perfect."

"Believe me, it is." She frowned at the darkening bruises, then squeezed the cloth, causing a stream of warm water to flow over his battered flesh. "You've saved my life three times in the past two days. I don't know how I'm ever going to be able to repay you."

Roarke sucked in a breath as the treacherous cloth dipped beneath the water and moved steadily lower, over his rib cage, his belly.

"Several ideas come to mind. And as tempted as I am to take what you're offering in exchange for continued protection, it isn't necessary. Because I'm sticking around for as long as it takes to get my story. Since keeping you safe seems to be the only way to do that, you don't owe me anything. Including sex."

Knowing how difficult it must have been for her to have agreed to a no-strings affair in the first place, Roarke felt exactly like the bastard he was as he viewed first the shock, then the humiliation move across her face. And then, watching the way she stiffened her shoulders, he felt even lower than a snake in a rut.

"I assume a big macho man like you can handle the rest by yourself."

Her words matched the coolness that had replaced the pain in her gilt eyes. He would have believed the ice-princess act was real if the slight trembling of her hand, as she held the washcloth out to him, hadn't given her away.

"I've been taking care of myself for a very long time."

"And you like it that way."

His gaze met her challenging one. "Got it on the first try."

"Fine." She threw the cloth against his chest, spun on her heel, and walked back out the door. She didn't really slam it, Roarke decided. But she came damn close.

Sighing, but knowing he'd done the right thing for both of them, he retrieved the washcloth from beneath the dissolving bubbles and scrubbed his body with a vengeance, hoping the pain would overcome another, far more primal.

9

ACCUSTOMED TO SOMETIMES having to go for days without sleep, Roarke was up before dawn. He went into the kitchen and started the coffee brewing. His original plan had been to leave the city before first light, but since she'd admittedly been through a lot, he'd decided Daria needed to sleep.

Sugar had arrived earlier with the van, which he'd left for Roarke and Daria to use. A woman detective had followed Sugar to the house and they'd left together in a nondescript Ford Taurus.

"That smells wonderful," Daria said as she entered the kitchen. She was wearing a pair of gray leggings and an oversize gray Loyola sweatshirt.

When he'd packed her things, Roarke had thought her wardrobe—which seemed to be mostly proper business suits—too understated for his taste. Her underwear, however, had been an entirely different story. As he'd gathered up the frothy confections the vandals hadn't destroyed, he'd decided that she must have bought out the entire lingerie department at Royal Street's famed Fleur de Paris. Incredibly, just wondering what she was wearing beneath that drab outfit made him hard.

He handed her a cup.

She took a sip, then sighed her appreciation. "And it tastes as good as it smells."

Her soft sigh and the way her eyes turned the hue of molten gold made him want to drag her down onto the kitchen table, or beneath it. When she looked up at him, saw the masculine desire in his dark gaze, she blushed and quickly lowered her eyes. When he found himself wanting to see if he could make her entire body flush, Roarke decided it was time—past time—to get back to the business at hand.

"How's your memory?"

Too vivid for comfort. As she recalled, with exquisite detail, the erotic dream she'd experienced just before waking, Daria felt the fever rise even hotter in her cheeks.

"I haven't remembered anything else about the murders."

"I have a plan to see if we can remedy that. If you're willing."

"Absolutely." She would do anything to banish the annoying fog that still hovered over part of her mind.

"It could be dangerous."

"Gee, that'll be a unique experience."

Her dry tone almost made him laugh. "Nothing like living on the edge to get the blood racing."

Her blood had certainly raced last night when she'd been bathing him. Before he'd sent her away. "I'm afraid I might be turning into an adrenaline junkie," she admitted.

"You could well be. But believe me, baby, it's a rough addiction to kick.

"By the way, Mike wants to send an artist over. To make a sketch of the murder victim you remember from the bayou."

The very thought sent a frisson of fear skimming up her spine. "All right." She didn't want to have to think about that, didn't want to remember the horror of watching that poor man die, but knew she had no choice.

"And then, after that's taken care of, I want to get you out of the city."

"Where? To another safe house?"

"Sort of. It's in the bayou." He'd no sooner said the word when Roarke saw her body stiffen.

"I've got a place I used to use for hunting and fishing," he explained. "We'll be safe there while Mike works the case on this end and we see how much of your memory returns."

"It's more than that, isn't it? You're hoping taking me out there might help me remember the faces of the men who shot that man."

His expression was as grim as her thoughts. "Yeah."

Daria was grateful to him for not trying to evade the truth, even though he had to know that she dreaded the very idea of returning to that place of nightmares.

"I'll go." The words were exhaled on a soft, shimmering sigh of surrender. She had no choice, Daria knew. Because something told her that the answer to all this could be found out in the dark, mysterious bayou swampland.

He'd known she would agree. Now Roarke could only hope that his admittedly risky plan wouldn't end up getting them both killed.

The former police artist was friendly, efficient and talented. He patiently drew and rejected features until he had pieced together a sketch that somewhat resembled Daria's recollection of the murdered man's face. But Daria was not satisfied. "It could be anyone," she muttered as she looked down at the composite drawing.

"You'd be surprised how helpful they can be," the man assured her. "And you did real good, Ms. Shea. That teardrop tattoo, for instance, suggests he'd killed someone. If he served time, we should be able to match him up to a mug shot."

Personally, Daria thought the odds were slim. Hopefully, Michael O'Malley would turn out to be as good a detective as Roarke kept saying he was. Because for that black-and-white sketch to be any help, he would have to be a combination of Sherlock Holmes, Columbo and Sam Spade.

"I wonder if it's someone I prosecuted," she murmured.

"It could be somebody you sent away," Roarke said at the same time.

They exchanged a look and Daria found herself being warmed by the first genuine smile he'd given her.

"That's a distinct possibility," the artist agreed as he sprayed the drawing with fixative, then put his charcoal pencil and paper tablet back into his leather case. "You could be looking at a gang killing." He turned to Roarke. "You gonna keep in touch?"

Roarke nodded. "Mike'll know how to get hold of me."

He walked the artist to the door, leaving Daria in the kitchen. She heard their murmured conversation and wondered if they were talking about her.

"Keith was once the local representative for the police union," Roarke said when he came back.

"Oh?" Realizing he was not a man prone to small talk, Daria wondered why he was telling her this.

"Funny thing." He refilled his coffee cup, then held

the carafe out to her. Her nerves were already jangling from having to recall what she'd seen in the bayou, and Daria turned him down with a shake of her head. "Turns out that the state organization contributed to your fiancé's campaign."

"That's not unusual. Candidates always try to get the endorsement of the local police unions."

"True enough. But this was a little different. Some of the brass made not-so-veiled suggestions that it might be beneficial for all concerned if the cops themselves contributed to the campaign."

"They threatened them?"

"I wouldn't put it that way." He took a drink, eyeing her over the rim of the cup, watching her for any sign of prevarication. If he'd paid more attention to Natasha that morning, she might still be alive. "Encouraged them to do their civic duty by electing a law-and-order candidate is probably a better way to put it."

"I can't believe people would be killed for not contributing to a campaign."

"That's a little Draconian. Even for Boudreaux," he admitted. "But they were skating on some very thin legal ice. What would you have done if you'd happened to run across illegal campaign contributions?"

"File charges," she said without hesitation.

"Against your own fiancé?"

"If he was breaking the law, I'd have no choice."

Roarke shook his head, thinking how simple the world would be if it consisted of absolutes—black and white, good guys and bad.

"I know what you're thinking," she said when he didn't immediately answer. "You believe I'm too old-fashioned. Too rigid."

"Louisiana isn't exactly known for its rigidity," he reminded.

"I know. And that's part of the problem. Not just here, but everywhere. People think that rules and laws don't matter anymore. They feel free to break them—maybe starting with the little ones, like speeding, or cheating on their taxes, and then pretty soon they're not paying child support and then—"

"It's a slippery slope to Angola," Roarke broke in.

"You don't have to laugh at me."

"I'm not. Not really." Because he wanted to kiss her, and that was just for starters, Roarke turned away and poured the rest of his coffee down the drain, then put the cup in the dishwasher. When he turned back to her, his expression was as serious as she'd ever seen it. "I admire you. But not many people would share your unwavering commitment to the law." Which meant that the suspect list could be a very long one.

"Believe me, I know that." She surprised him by laughing. "Otherwise, I'd have a one-hundred-percent conviction rate."

She stared at him. "Roarke..."

He didn't say a word. Just stood there, waiting for the memory to come into focus.

"Damn." She covered her face with her hands. "I was so close."

He hated seeing her so distressed. "It'll come," he assured her yet again.

Because he was beginning to care for her in a way that could only complicate things, he knew that to raise the level of intimacy would be even more dangerous this morning than it had been last night. He was too much like his father—he was a rover, a man incapable of settling down in one place, with one woman.

Life had made him cynical; experience had made him unwilling to trust anyone, with the exception of his brother. An intelligent, levelheaded woman like Daria Shea shouldn't want him but, amazed that she did, he pulled her hands away from her lovely, troubled face and lowered his mouth to hers.

Unlike the unbridled passion she'd sensed before, Roarke's kiss was light as a feather and surprisingly tender. And it still possessed the power to make Daria's toes curl in her sneakers. And, she feared, to break her heart.

She looked up at him when the brief gentle kiss ended. "What was that for?"

"For you." He smiled and touched his fingertips to her cheek. "And for me."

They exchanged a long look.

"We'd better get going," he said finally.

As she left the house with him, Daria understood that in that silent, suspended moment, things between them had shifted yet again.

ROARKE KNEW THAT to many people, the word *swamp* conjured up unattractive images of snakes and gas and gators. Yet although he'd traveled to every corner of the globe, he'd never found a place as enchanting as Louisiana's freshwater, forested bayous.

He suspected that all those people who so readily vilified the gloriously soggy acres that made up America's largest swamp ecosystem didn't realize that its rookeries were home to thousands of birds and in spring, the myriad unnamed lakes vanished in a dazzling display of flowers.

As much as he loved the city, for some reason, from the time his uncle had first taken him hunting in the Atchafalaya River Basin, it had become one of the few places he'd ever felt truly at peace.

"There's a part of me that thinks I should be terrified," Daria mused aloud as they drove through the vast fields of wetlands. "Considering the horrible thing I remember that happened out here."

Since it was the first thing she'd said since they'd left New Orleans nearly an hour earlier, Roarke glanced over at her. "I hear a but in that statement."

"A stronger part of me can't help being calmed by the almost-surreal beauty." She'd no sooner spoken than a giant heron took flight from the bayou bank in a graceful flurry of blue-gray wings.

It figured she would understand the mysterious land's charm. Everything about the woman just kept pulling him in deeper. She hadn't even complained about the eau de crayfish permeating the van. "The bayou's not for everyone."

"Thank goodness. After we crossed the bridge, I remembered working on a murder case where the suspect came from Houma. I spent a lot of time out here and fell in love."

"Hopefully not with the suspect."

She smiled at that. "No. With the land itself. It's not the kind of love that hits like a lightning bolt—it sneaks up on you, fills empty places inside you that you never knew existed. After I left, I realized I'd taken a bit of it with me."

She charmed him by blushing yet again. "I'm sorry. I realize that sounds hopelessly romantic, but—"

"It's true."

Roarke was tempted to ask her to marry him on the

spot. She was too damn perfect. For his own safety, he was going to have to find some flaw or he was sunk.

"The tourists go out in the commercial boats, see a few nutria, maybe watch the guide feed an alligator a piece of raw chicken from a fishing pole, eat some boiled crayfish spiced up with Tabasco sauce and believe they've been to the bayou.

"But it's not that kind of place. You can't drive up to it, take a few quick snapshots, then roar off again to the plantation tour, or the French Quarter, or on to Memphis to visit Elvis's grave. It's a wandering place."

"Maybe that's why you love it so," Daria said. "Because it *is* a wandering place. And, given your career, you're obviously a man with wanderlust in his blood."

Just like his father. How many times had Roarke heard his mother accuse him of that? The difference was, Roarke decided, that although Patrick O'Malley continued to roam the world, taking his Pulitzer prize-winning news photographs, his middle son, at least, was beginning to get weary of chasing after something that always seemed just out of reach.

Not prepared to share his recent doubts about the direction his life had taken with this woman he'd already allowed to get too close, Roarke merely nodded and said, "You may have a point."

There was something there, Daria mused, studying him surreptitiously as she pretended great interest in the acres of rice fields they were driving through. Watching the way his eyes narrowed and his jaw clenched at her seemingly innocent statement, she couldn't help wondering if perhaps Roarke O'Malley hadn't spent the last ten years of his life running not *to* something, but *from* something.

As if deciding they'd talked long enough, Roarke reached out, turned on the van's radio and tuned it to a local FM station. Daria listened to the plaintive Cajun song and, although she could comprehend less than half of the regional patois, the depressing story of a love gone tragically wrong came through all too clearly. Since she already had enough to feel glum about, she was relieved when it was followed by a brighter, jaunty tune about crayfish pie and jambalaya.

A comfortable silence settled over them as they continued deeper and deeper into the bayou. Knowing how the landscape always changed, how watercourses could become flats, how seemingly solid land could be turned into rushing water in the spring, how drowned land was reborn over and over again, Daria wondered how on earth Roarke knew where he was headed.

But strangely, although she'd gotten the impression that he didn't come home often, he seemed to be zeroing in on his destination with the instincts of a homing pigeon. In the distance, under the winter-pale sky, thunderheads rose like dark iron anvils.

They passed a cemetery, the graves built aboveground, as they were back in the city, to prevent the bodies from floating to the surface. The glint of sun on a broken angel's wing triggered a flash of memory.

"Roarke!" She grabbed his arm, almost causing the van to veer off the narrow road.

"What?" He cursed mildly under his breath as he corrected the steering.

"I just remembered something."

He immediately pulled over to the shoulder and cut the engine. He'd been hoping this trip would trigger something and was pleased it was already paying off.

"After I left you outside the hotel, I was running through the Quarter and had reached Armstrong Park when a man in an executioner's hood caught up with me."

Hell. "I remember seeing that guy." Roarke's hands curved into fists as he pictured the man who'd run past him in the other direction.

"He pulled me into the cemetery and threatened to take me out into the bayou, which made me realize he was going to kill me, so I tried offering him something that might change his mind."

"What?" Thinking he was about to learn what the rogue cops had trashed her house trying to find, Roarke was not expecting her next words.

"Me."

"You?" He dragged his hand through his hair and stared at her. "Are you nuts?"

She lifted her chin defiantly. "I didn't feel I had any choice. And I certainly wasn't planning to actually go through with it. I was just stalling for time."

"Terrific plan, Nancy Drew." His sarcastic tone said otherwise.

"The point is, it worked. I distracted him long enough to get away. I remember scooping my purse from the ground—for some reason it seemed important at the time—then noticing that it had come open. That's the last thing I remember."

It wasn't much. But it was more than they'd had earlier. "I'll get Mike working on it." The van, which was obviously more than just a fish-delivery truck, was outfitted with a cellular phone. Roarke punched in his brother's office number.

"I'll have some people start checking out the cemetery right away," Michael said without hesitation when Roarke passed on Daria's latest recollection. "See what we can find, although anything of any value would already have been snatched up. We'll also go over Louis Armstrong Park with a fine-tooth comb and track the way to where you found her. There's always the chance that she lost it on the street, which means the cleaning crews would already have swept it up. Whatever it is."

"Maybe we'll get lucky and it'll have dropped out in the cemetery," Roarke said.

"I'll burn a candle to Marie Laveaux."

Despite the seriousness of the situation, Roarke laughed at his brother's dryly stated offer. "Thanks, Mike. I owe you."

"Hey, that's what brothers are for." That said, Michael hung up.

"It's probably nothing," Daria murmured.

"And it could be exactly what we need to break the case," Roarke countered. "Besides, it's more to go on than we had five minutes ago."

That was true. As she settled back into the seat and watched the magnificent scenery flash by the passenger window, Daria hoped that being out here in the bayou—which had proved so horrifying when her would-be killer had threatened her with it—would stimulate even more memories.

The afternoon sun was slanting low on the horizon when Roarke turned off the single-lane dirt road and cut across the quaking land. Five minutes later, he stopped in front of small dock. A flat-bottomed boat was tied up at the dock.

"We're going out in a boat?"

She hadn't agreed to this. It would make her much more vulnerable. And definitely under his control.

"It's either that or swim."

As she got out of the car and glanced back at the way they'd come, Daria knew that she would never be able to find her way back to civilization. She'd opted to trust him; the only thing to do was to stick to that decision.

She didn't answer, but climbed into the boat and settled down on a wooden seat with a regal air. Roarke thought she looked exactly how Princess Di would look if she ever suddenly decided to drop by the bayou for a ride in his mud boat. Restraining a grin, he retrieved their suitcases from the van.

As he started the engine and pulled away from the dock, Daria felt as if she'd cast her fate to the winds. She was at the mercy of this handsome-as-sin stranger who frazzled her nerves and made her feel hot and cold all at the same time.

As the boat skimmed across the water, edging through the shallows, the only sound was the drone of the inboard motor, and even that stopped when they reached a place that was more mud than water. Worried that they would be forced to spend the night in this smoky, spooky place, Daria was relieved when Roarke picked up a long pole from the bottom of the boat and began expertly maneuvering them through the marsh. Toward their destination. Wherever that was.

While the boat drifted through the towering cypress trees, a deep silence settled over them. Nothing was as quiet as a swamp. Especially during this twilit time between day and night.

As civilization slowly disappeared behind them, Daria found herself almost forgetting her reason for coming out here. She felt her entire body relax—neck, shoulders, spine. In this place that was both melancholy and comforting at the same time, her mind began to drift like the slow-moving current flowing inexorably to the Gulf. Somewhere in the far distance, someone was playing "Jolie Blonde" on an accordion.

They passed a small sign nailed to a huge cypress: Oil and Gas Pipeline. Do Not Anchor or Dredge.

"My father was an oil-company executive," she said suddenly.

Roarke glanced over at her, pleased that more of her memory was returning, but wishing it had more to do with the case. "Mike's been trying to locate your family. But he hasn't had any luck."

"That's because I'm an only child. And my parents were killed in a plane crash in the Rockies the winter before I graduated from college."

Roarke supposed that explained her strong independent streak. When you didn't have anyone to lean on, you'd better learn to stand on your own two feet.

"Did you grow up in Colorado?"

"No. I was born in New Orleans, but I was sent away to private schools in Europe. Dad's work involved so much traveling, my parents felt it'd be better for me to grow up in a more stable environment. It was in Switzerland," she remembered, envisioning the crystal lakes and snowclad Alps.

Roarke thought about the noisy house filled with brothers and aunts and uncles and cousins he'd grown up in. "Sounds lonely."

She sighed. "It was. And cold. I remember when I was fourteen, trying to talk my parents into letting me transfer to a school in Hawaii, but my father was afraid I'd spend all my time hanging out on Waikiki with surfers, sailors and beach bums."

"I think most fathers of fourteen-year-old girls would probably worry about that."

She grinned at the memory of the arguments that had raged via transatlantic lines for days. "The annoying thing is that, although I hate to admit it, he was probably right."

"So he kept you in the protective custody of a convent of nuns."

"Until I was paroled to go to Stanford."

"Where you made up for lost time?"

She thought about that for a minute. Then shook her head. "Not really. In fact, I was considered pretty much a geek. I always had my nose in a book and since I'd spent so many years living in a totally female environment, I had no idea how to talk to boys."

Roarke thought back to their first meeting in the bar. "Obviously sometime between then and when you picked me up in the Blue Bayou, you've learned a few tricks of the trade."

Since his half smile took the sarcasm out of his tone, Daria didn't take offense. "I suppose I have. Then again, maybe you were just easy."

This time he flashed a full-blown smile that bathed her in its warmth. "Honey, the one thing no one has ever called me is 'easy.'"

Now that, Daria could believe.

When the narrow mudflat opened back into a riverway, Roarke put the pole away and returned to using the engine. Dusk was settling in long silvery-pink fingers that caused an otherworldly glow to spill over the landscape.

They came around a bend and suddenly the river opened onto what seemed to be a secret lake. Located on the banks of the lake, beneath the limbs of a huge spreading oak tree hundreds of years old was an old-style planter's cabin set on stilts.

The cabin, which boasted a front porch and an outside stairway to the *garçonnière*, a place beneath the roof that had originally been designed for the young men of the large families to sleep. The sun was setting quickly into the water now, draping the cabin in shadows that resembled the Spanish moss hanging from the cypress trees all around the place. The cottage had been built in a location isolated even by bayou standards.

"I don't want to sound picky," Daria said tentatively as he guided the boat up to the dock, knowing all too well the wildlife that made their home in these waters, "but how long has it been since anyone's been in here?"

He glanced back over his shoulder as he cut the engine. "What's the matter? Got a problem sharing your quarters with cottonmouths?"

"It seems I already have enough two-legged snakes in my life," she said. "I'm not exactly eager for more."

He laughed at that. "Don't worry. Mike uses it a lot as a getaway. And my Uncle Claude comes in every so often to beat back the wildlife. I called him before I left Moscow, and he said he'd get the place fixed up and the pantry stocked for me."

Daria didn't bother to conceal her relief. Or her embarrassment. "I'm sorry. I realize you probably think I'm a nervous female, but—"

"Shut up." When he leaned toward her, Daria braced herself for another kiss, but he merely brushed his lips against her forehead. "You're one of the bravest people I've ever met."

The compliment shouldn't have meant so much. But it did. "Really?"

Her radiant smile warmed the glacier that had taken hold of his heart even before that debacle in Moscow. Roarke had learned early on in his career that if you allowed yourself to care too much, the pain could eat you alive. Some war correspondents drank heavily to forget the horrors they witnessed firsthand. Others tended to overindulge in sex or drugs. A few opted for suicide.

The day Roarke had discovered the ABC reporter who'd become a mentor of sorts hanging from a rafter in a shelled-out building in Beirut, the first sheeting of ice had coated his heart as a self-defense mechanism. Over the years the ice had thickened and although it had developed fissures from time to time, never had it been in such danger of melting.

"You're also crazy." Because he wanted to kiss her—worse yet, *needed* to kiss her—Roarke backed away. "Did you ever think that coming out here in the middle of nowhere with a total stranger could get you killed?"

"Not for a minute." Her smile vanished, her expression turned as sober as he'd ever seen it. He could see the lines of strain on a face as pale and translucent as the petals of a water hyacinth. "Not with you."

She truly was the most reckless woman he'd ever met. Or she really was nuts. Either way, she triggered something unwanted deep inside him, beneath the ice. It was, Roarke realized, the determination of a male to protect his mate. Whatever the cost.

Their eyes met, his dark and filled with warning, hers soft and trusting, but laced with a steely determination. Roarke felt powerless against her alluring combination of passion and fragility. He tried to remind himself yet again that the lady was not his type. Despite her assertion that she was willing to settle for a hot, short-lived affair, Roarke knew Daria was the "forever after" kind of woman. Like his mother.

He'd grown up watching the emotional pain and loneliness Mary O'Malley had endured as the wife of globe-trotting photojournalist Patrick O'Malley. When he'd chosen a similarly rootless career path, Roarke had made the decision not to get enmeshed in deep emotional relationships.

His hit-and-run style had always suited him perfectly. Just as it had suited lovers chosen for their own carefree attitude toward sex. Women willing to move on to other countries, other conflicts, other men, when their time together had run its course.

Feeling as if he'd stumbled into quicksand, Roarke was debating taking Daria back to the city, straight to the federal building, where he probably should have taken her in the first place. But suddenly, what had been merely a low, threatening rumble on the horizon became a vicious crack directly overhead. Seconds later, the sky opened up and rain began pouring down on them.

10

ROARKE TUCKED THEIR suitcases under one arm and together they ran the short distance to the steps leading up to the raised porch. By the time they entered the main room of the cabin, they were both drenched.

The room was as dark as the inside of a tomb. And just as quiet. The only sounds were the rat-a-tat of the rain on the tin roof and the cracks of thunder. Lightning lit up the room in sulphurous flashes that reminded Daria of strobe lights.

"You're wet clear through to the skin," he said, running his hands over her shoulders and down her arms.

"So are you." She did the same thing to him.

"I don't have electricity out here, but there's a propane tank out back that supplies gas for heat, hot water, the stove and refrigerator. I could run you a bath." His hands slipped beneath her sweatshirt and cupped her breasts. "Or, if you don't want to wait all that time, we can try to create a little heat on our own."

They were already doing that. Daria could feel the little flames licking at her blood. Unwilling to play coy, she began unbuttoning his shirt, and was appalled to see that the bruises had turned such a deep, ugly purple, they looked almost black.

"Are you sure you're up to this?" When she

touched one particularly dark spot on his ribs she felt his involuntary intake of breath.

He took hold of her wrist and moved his hand downward, over his battered ribs, his taut belly, to his waist, then lower still. "The day I'm not up to taking a beautiful woman to bed," he murmured, "is the day they stick me in the Broussard family tomb."

"Broussard?" He was hard as forged steel beneath her palm, but even as Daria's blood beat faster and hotter, her natural curiosity was piqued. "But your name's O'Malley."

"That's my father's name. My mama's one-hundred-percent Cajun. In fact, this used to be Broussard land before my granddaddy left it to go to work in the salt mines on Jefferson Island. He took his family into town, which was where my mama met my daddy when he came south to photograph a story about the oil boom."

He thought about the story he'd heard all his life, how both his parents had felt as if they'd been hit by lightning. And how his mother had been pregnant when they'd married. Michael had been born nine months to the day of their first meeting, but Patrick O'Malley, on assignment at Cape Canaveral photographing the launch of the Mercury capsule *Freedom 7*, which had put America's first man into space, had missed the birth. As he had the subsequent arrival of his two younger sons.

"What's wrong?" Watching the dark scowl move across Roarke's face, Daria reached out with her free hand and touched his cheek.

"Nothing," he said brusquely. Nothing that he wanted to go into right now. "Your teeth are beginning to chatter. I'd better start a fire." Without giving her a chance to argue, he went back out onto the covered porch and gathered up some wood from the stack his uncle had obviously left for him.

Daria wrapped her arms around herself—partly to ward off the cold, partly in an unconscious gesture of self-protection against his rebuff. She watched him stack the wood in the black stove that, with the doors open, also served as a fireplace. His normally lithe movements seemed more deliberate. Stiffer than usual. Which wasn't surprising, considering yesterday's beating.

"Are you hurting?"

"Yeah. But not in the way you mean." Surrendering to the inevitable, he caught hold of the hem of her wet sweatshirt and yanked it over her head. "I'm hurting in a way only you can make better."

Daria gasped with pleasure as he deftly undid her bra, tossed it aside, then pulled her against him. His crisp chest hair against her bare breasts was one of the most erotic sensations she'd ever felt.

Remembering how he'd felt when he'd believed that he was about to die without ever having made love to Daria and tired of playing games, he pulled her down onto the fur rug in front of the fire.

"I thought you said this would be a mistake," she murmured.

"I did. I also recall saying that I've made a lot of mistakes in my life. So one more probably isn't going to make that much of a difference."

Gazing up at the hunger in his dark stormy eyes, Daria ignored the fact that she was not accustomed to having sex with men she'd picked up in bars, and completely overlooked the fact that she was an engaged woman.

All she knew was that if she didn't let Roarke make love to her, if she didn't allow herself to make love to him, she would regret the loss every day for the rest of her life.

"I think about you all the time," he murmured as he touched his mouth to the hollow of her throat. "Even yesterday, when those thugs were beating the hell out of me."

She tilted her head back, reveling in the heated touch of his lips and tongue. "I thought about you, too. I was so worried you were going to be killed."

"That thought passed through my mind." While his mouth roamed back down to create havoc on her breasts, his hands slipped beneath the waistband of the wet leggings. "In fact, there was a moment there, just when I thought I was about to die, that my entire life actually passed in front of my eyes, just like in the movies. And you know the only thing I truly regretted?"

His wicked, clever fingers were stroking her in a way that had her squirming against his hand. "What?" she managed on a ragged moan.

"That I might die without having made love to you." He bent his head and took a breast in his mouth, and sucked deeply.

"I know the feeling." She arched against him, felt his unmistakable hardness and felt a damp warmth gathering in that hot, burning place between her thighs.

"Tell me what you want, Daria." He was rocking against her, the wet denim scraping against her in a way she was surprised didn't create sparks.

"You." She clutched at him, her fingernails digging into his back. "I want you."

It was part plea, part surrender. And all truth. Daria wanted to feel his mouth against her fiery flesh; she yearned to take him deep inside her, to surround him, embrace him, to have him satisfy the tension that was drawing her entire body into an ever-tightening knot. Desire, thick and smoky, ruled her thoughts; passion, hot and ravenous, ruled her body.

It was all he needed to hear. All he'd been waiting to hear. He heard the voice in the back of his mind trying to remind him that he'd been in this deadly situation before, and ignored it.

He dragged the wet leggings and panties down her legs and flung them aside. Then, rocking back on his heels, he took hold of her ankles and spread her legs, offering the most intimate part of her feminine body to his view.

"Lovely," he murmured, as those wicked fingers skimmed over the outer lips rosy from the heated blood that had flowed from her heart into the tingling flesh. "Like rose petals. Smooth and soft and glistening with early-morning dew." His gaze met hers, and he watched the unmasked desire rise in her remarkable eyes as he parted those tender pink lips.

The fur was soft against her back as she lay there, as helpless and exposed as she'd ever been. But Daria was neither afraid nor embarrassed as she watched him watching her with unblinking intent.

The tension built deep inside her as he slipped his finger into her. When a second finger joined the first, and probed deeply, she began to squirm, then caught herself.

"Don't." He lowered his mouth to her breast and closed his teeth around her nipple. "Don't hold back, sweetheart. I want it all." His words were muffled against her flesh, but Daria had no trouble discerning his meaning. Flinging away the last of her restraint, she began to move against him, seeking relief to her escalating need.

All it took was the touch of his thumb against her ul-trasensitive clitoris to make her come. Feeling her in-ner spasms, Roarke paused his intimate stroking, to enjoy her orgasm. When the convulsions began to subside, he put his wide hand beneath her bottom, lifted her off the rug and pressed his mouth against the soft, swollen flesh between her thighs, savoring her taste as a man would enjoy the flavor of a ripe, juicy peach.

Daria cried out when she climaxed again, and would have pulled away, but Roarke refused to per-mit her to rest. He drove her higher and higher with lips and teeth and tongue. The low, rough sounds she was making deep in her throat as he brought her to or-gasm after orgasm caused his own hunger to flare even hotter.

The wind rattled the windows, howling like dark spirits around the cabin. The rain continued to ham-mer on the roof and the thunderous booms echoed those of Daria's pounding heart as the storm inside her raged even more wildly than the one outside.

"Roarke," she gasped as she clung to his shoulders. "I can't..."

"Yes, you can." He closed his teeth around a stone-hard nipple, wetted it with his tongue as he slipped a hand between them and proved her wrong. His own body felt on the verge of exploding, but he wasn't about to stop until he'd wrung every last ounce of pas-sion from her.

Daria had never imagined that such passion existed, had never known that she was capable of such uninhibited response. She cried out—in anguish, not in ecstasy—as he released her and stood, depriving her needy body of the power of his touch, his strength.

She wanted to complain, but the words would not come. She was in his power, helpless to resist, willing to do whatever he wanted, desperate to go wherever he took her.

She watched as he finally stripped off his own wet clothes, then lay down beside her again, pulled her to him and filled her, claiming her as she knew no man had ever done before.

Her shattering climax was instantaneous. Seized by tremors, her cry reverberating around the warming room, she clutched at him, afraid that if she wasn't somehow anchored, she would go spinning off the edge of the world.

Fired by her uninhibited response, Roarke's own tautly reined-in control snapped. Maneuvering them so that they were lying facing one another on their sides, her top leg high on his hip, he drove into her like a jackhammer, harder, deeper, until they came together in a mind-blinding explosion.

Neither Roarke nor Daria could speak. Neither moved. They lay there, breathing heavily, gasping for breath, arms and legs entangled on the fur rug for what could have been minutes. Or an eternity.

It was Roarke who finally broke the silence. "I'm sorry. I shouldn't have done that."

"What?" She'd been thinking that they had, indeed, lived up to his promise of "world-class."

"I shouldn't have taken you on the floor like some wild man."

"Oh, I think I liked that." She smiled up at him. "I

take it back. I *know* I liked that." Her smile widened, lighting up her eyes. In the glow from the nearby fire he saw tiny twins of himself in her pupils. "I feel absolutely ravished."

He pushed some wet strands of hair away from her flushed face. "You know, it is possible to be ravished in a bed."

Personally, Daria wasn't sure she would ever be able to move again. And she was certain that she'd used up at least a month's quota of orgasms. "Surely you don't mean..." Her voice drifted off as she felt him beginning to swell inside her. "Roarke, you may be an iron man, but I couldn't possibly—"

His dark head swooped down and he cut off her protest with a deep hard kiss that threatened to steal what little breath she had left in her lungs.

"Want to bet?"

Gently unwinding their arms and legs, he lifted her from the rug and carried her into the adjoining bedroom, where he laid her down on the soft mattress stuffed with dried Spanish moss and proceeded to kiss her senseless.

As the storm moved on and a full white moon rose over the bayou, Roarke proceeded to demonstrate exactly how much Daria had underestimated her aptitude for passion.

THE CABIN BEDROOM was cloaked in a silvery predawn light when Roarke awoke. The pain that had been held at bay by his sexual hunger now throbbed in every muscle of his body. And he hadn't had such a headache since the night he'd gotten into an ouzo-drinking contest in Athens with a UPI reporter.

He also realized he'd made the biggest mistake of

his life. And, after the Moscow fiasco, that was really saying something.

He looked down at Daria, who was sleeping in his arms. Her hair had dried into wild waves that felt like silk ribbons against his chest, her lashes were thick and black on her cheeks, and the slight shadows beneath her closed lids revealed a lack of sleep. The beard-reddened skin on her cheeks and breasts was evidence of exactly how she'd spent that sleepless night.

She looked as innocent as a newborn fawn. Which he'd decided she was. During their long, love-filled night, she'd opened for him completely, had held nothing back. She was nothing like Natasha, who'd used sex as a means first of enticement, then control.

Unlike Natasha, Daria had willingly surrendered all control to Roarke. He suspected that there had been nothing he could have asked her to do that she wouldn't have willingly done; no secrets he could have insisted she reveal that she wouldn't have told him. She was, amazingly, one of those rare individuals absolutely without guile.

Which was what made her career choice so surprising. And also explained why so many people were out to kill her. Mike had said she was both fearless and relentless when prosecuting the bad guys. She'd already succeeded in bringing down those crooked judges; this time, it seemed she'd zeroed in on someone who was not willing to spend time behind bars. The fact that a federal attorney had been involved was even more proof that whoever she was after was high up in Louisiana's power hierarchy.

Such integrity was to be admired, even though he

personally found it foolhardy. Unfortunately, he'd proved himself to be far less honorable.

Roarke was not feeling guilty about having spent the night having sex with Daria Shea. He was, after all, a normal male with normal desires. And what man wouldn't be fascinated and intrigued to discover that a woman whose closet was full of prim little dress-for-success suits possessed such a deep core of primitive passion?

The mistake had been not once thinking of protection. And even as he tried to blame his mental lapse on the beating he'd taken, Roarke knew that it wasn't the thugs who had made him forget what had been an elemental part of his sexual behavior since his early teens. It was Daria. She had clouded his mind just as she'd caused his body to burn with a shimmering white heat.

But even as he tried to blame her, he knew the responsibility rested solely on his battered shoulders—as would whatever outcome that might occur from such a stupid, careless lapse in judgment.

As if the intensity of his thoughts had managed to filter through her consciousness, Daria's eyes fluttered open and she found herself looking directly into Roarke's eyes. They were the dark blue of a storm-tossed sea, which echoed the grim, tight line of those lips that had created such wondrous havoc over every inch of her body during the seemingly endless night.

"Good morning." Although she was picking up disturbing vibrations from him, she managed a faint, self-conscious smile.

Still furious with himself, Roarke answered with a smile that was a parody of the warm ones he'd given her last night. "I owe you an apology."

Well, Daria thought with a sigh, that was what she got for succumbing to a one-night stand with a man she didn't really know. What had she expected? A heartfelt proposal of everlasting love?

She'd no sooner asked herself that rhetorical question when, as ridiculous as it seemed, she realized the answer was *yes*.

"We've already been through that. You don't owe me any apology, Roarke." She tried for a calm, matter-of-fact tone, but her words came out soft and edged with a vulnerability she hated to hear in her voice. "I wanted you to make—" she practically bit her tongue as she stopped just short of saying the fatal *L* word. "I wanted to have sex with you."

"Sex is one thing. Parenthood another."

"Parenthood?" She looked up at him, surprised. Then his meaning sank in. "Oh." She hitched herself up in bed and feeling uncomfortably naked, pulled the sheet up over her bare breasts. "You don't have to worry. I'm on the Pill."

He lifted a brow. "Funny you should remember that."

"I didn't. I found the pills in my purse. Surely, since you searched it, you must have seen them, too."

"You could have missed one. Or more. Your life has been a bit unsettled lately," he said with dry understatement.

"Granted," she admitted.

"And there's a lot more to worry about these days than an unexpected pregnancy."

"True again." This time her expression was as glum as his.

"You don't have to worry about any diseases. The

network increased my life insurance before I left for Moscow. I passed the physical with flying colors."

"James and I had physicals before we got our marriage license two weeks ago," she recalled. "I'm fine, as well."

"Then I guess we don't have anything to worry about," he said.

"No," she said quietly. Sadly, he thought. "I guess we don't."

A silence settled over them. A pregnant silence, Roarke thought grimly. "Those pills aren't one-hundred-percent accurate. If anything happens, I want you to know I won't ditch my responsibility."

Was he actually offering to marry her if she ended up pregnant? No, Daria decided. He was merely assuring her he would help with the expenses, which, given the news reports of his last contract negotiations, he could certainly afford to do.

"That isn't necessary."

He caught the thrust-out jaw between his fingers. "I said I'd do my part."

When she tried to toss her head, his fingers tightened. "Fine." Her voice and her eyes were ice.

Deciding he liked her better when she was warm and trembling in his arms, Roarke slowly lowered his head. "Good. And now that we've got that settled..."

"Roarke..." She sighed as his lips feathered soft little kisses against hers. "I can't believe that after last night you'd still want this."

"Me, neither." Once again the pain that had been racking his body faded away as desire rose. "But God help me, I do." *God help them both.* His hand nudged between them, deftly locating the warm damp place between her thighs. "And, so, it seems, do you."

"I know." Her body was melting, like wax in a hot July New Orleans sun. "I can't seem to help myself where you're concerned."

"I know how that feels." He rolled over onto his back and pulled her on top of him. "Too well."

Their lips met and clung, their bodies fit together as if they'd been designed solely with each other in mind. And as the stuttering winter sun rose over the bayou, Roarke and Daria rose with it.

"WOULD YOU LIKE some more wine, Congressman?"

James Boudreaux looked up into the smiling face of the flight attendant. She'd been hovering over him since he'd first walked through the door of the airliner, offering him hot towels, drinks and food. Her name was Heather. She'd been working the first-class section on the D.C.-to-New Orleans route for some time and had spent more than one layover in Washington in his bed. Lately he'd gotten the impression that she'd been angling to become Mrs. Boudreaux.

Which, of course, wasn't going to happen in this lifetime. He'd had his life planned from the time he'd entered seventh grade at the Longfellow middle school: a brief term in the state legislature, two terms in the U.S. Congress, then a senate seat that would launch his move into the White House. These past years, being considered one of Washington's most eligible bachelors had garnered him a great deal of publicity, but his pollsters had determined a senator needed to appear more stable, more of a devoted family man. Which was why he'd proposed to Daria Shea.

She didn't have any family to interfere with their lives; she was attractive, intelligent and would undoubtedly make a good mother to the children that would provide the last all-important detail to his public persona before he made his move to be elected president.

The problem was, he'd made the mistake of overlooking exactly how seriously she took her career. She was adamant about keeping her damn job as a prosecutor and she refused to understand that by constantly irritating the powers-that-be in the state—no one in his memory had actually dared indict a sitting judge—she was endangering his future, as well.

The moneymen had warned him she was becoming a liability. Enough so that he'd decided to break things off. Then when she'd begun investigating the Tribunal, he'd thought that by marrying her he could prevent her from testifying against him in the event his part in the group became known. But after she'd witnessed that murder, and discovered that he was the leader of the men who'd taken it upon themselves to dispense justice when the system failed, he'd realized that Daria Shea had to be eliminated. And now, it appeared, he was going to have the pleasure of finally settling things with his childhood nemesis, as well.

He would make O'Malley beg, James decided. Then crawl. Oh, yes, he thought with a rush of pleasure that was almost sexual, he was going to enjoy breaking Roarke O'Malley.

He smiled up at the pretty brunette holding the bottle of Cabernet Sauvignon. "Thank you, darlin'," he said, resisting the urge to run his hand up her smooth thigh. "I believe I would enjoy another glass."

When she bent down to refill his glass, which put her bouncy breasts right at eye level, James regretted that business was going to prevent him from enjoying what she was so obviously offering.

Perhaps, he considered as he sipped his wine, he would have sex with Daria one last time. Although he'd never been able to excite her, perhaps part of the problem was that he'd always treated her too carefully.

Fear might loosen her up. And a little pain might even melt some of that damn ice she'd encased herself in. That was what he would do, James decided. He would let his men knock her around a little, just to warm her up. Then he would take her, hard and rough.

And then, after he'd finally gotten Daria Shea to scream, he would kill her.

The idea made him smile. The thirty-something woman across the aisle, thinking the smile was meant for her, smiled back.

11

DARIA SAT OUT on the porch of the cabin, her feet up on the railing, drinking the coffee Roarke had brewed, reveling in the restful stillness of the bayou morning. The storm had passed and the bright rays of the morning sunlight shafting through the trees glistened like liquid gold on the still, dark water.

At first glance, the bayou was so serene she felt as if she and Roarke could have been the only living things in the world. But gradually, she began to notice the white egrets on a distant bank dining on a breakfast of minnows, while nearby, a family of white-tailed deer grazed peacefully on the marsh grass. A pair of nutria swam by, so close she could have reached out and touched them; a squirrel ran in circles up a cypress tree beside the cabin, chattering furiously; flocks of wintering ducks floated by and bullfrogs croaked.

"This is almost worth it," she murmured as she heard him open the screen door and come out onto the porch behind her.

He bent down and kissed the top of her head. "What's that?"

"Being here in this magical place almost makes up for everything that's happened to me in the past few days." She glanced up at him and smiled, her heart in her eyes. "And being here with you makes it even more special."

He knew exactly what she meant. Because he felt the same way himself. Even so, Roarke felt obliged to remind her that they weren't here on a vacation.

"I take it being in the bayou hasn't triggered any memories of that murder you witnessed?"

She sighed. Even knowing he was right to bring the subject back to their reason for being here, Daria didn't want reality to intrude on the pleasure she was feeling. Not quite yet.

"How can I remember anything so horrible?" she asked quietly, "when my mind's filled with the glorious way you make me feel?"

If there was ever a time to take off running, Roarke thought, this was it. She wasn't just wearing her heart on her sleeve, it was gleaming in her remarkable golden eyes.

Dragging his gaze from hers, he sat down in the creaky wicker chair next to her and put his feet up on the railing beside hers. As he watched a raccoon washing its morning meal in the water on a nearby bank, Roarke allowed himself the perilous fantasy of just staying out here with Daria forever.

"I can't quite get a handle on you," he grumbled.

She glanced over at him, surprised. "I haven't held anything back." That was definitely true. Especially last night. "Not that I remember, anyway."

"I'm not accusing you of that." He continued to look out over the water. "It's just that you seem so open and it would seem to me that a prosecutor needs to keep his—or her—cards pretty close to the chest."

She thought about that and allowed that he had a point. "Perhaps that's how I got into trouble in the first place."

"That's pretty much the conclusion I've come to."

Unable to resist touching her, he reached out and stroked her thigh, clad this morning in black leggings. "I've also been wondering if perhaps something more than just that graze to the head is blocking your memory."

"What do you mean?"

"What if whatever you witnessed was so emotionally traumatic that your mind couldn't handle it?"

"Murder's ugly," she agreed. "But I deal with it every day."

"Speaking of that, Mike's checking out the cases you've worked on during the past few months to see if he can uncover anything that might have ticked off some of the powers that be. If there's any pattern, he'll find it."

"But how will you find out what, if anything, he discovers?" The phone in the van hadn't been portable and needless to say, no one had gone to the trouble of stringing up phone lines all the way out here.

"There's a bait shop a few miles from here, about twenty minutes by boat. There's a phone I can use to call him. And to hook up to my laptop modem. He promised to E-mail me some files."

"I suppose it goes without saying that we can trust Michael." Daria couldn't quite keep the question from her tone.

A flinty warning appeared in his dark blue eyes. "Unequivocally."

It was enough for her. Daria nodded. "You're lucky, having brothers."

"I've always thought so. At least when they weren't beating me up."

"They beat you up?"

He shrugged. "When we were kids, we fought all the time. It wasn't any big deal."

She thought about that. "I guess it's a guy thing."

He shrugged again, but she didn't miss the grin tugging at the corner of his mouth. "I guess so."

They sat there for a while longer, each content to simply enjoy the company of the other. When a boat approached, she felt Roarke tense beside her. Daria was halfway out of her chair when he said, "Don't worry. It's just my Uncle Claude, checking his traps."

"His traps?"

"It's crayfish season. From the height of the water, it'll be a good year, which is lucky for Claude, since Mike told me our Aunt Evangeline is pregnant with her sixth."

"That's quite a lot of mouths to feed."

"It's a helluva lot of crayfish," Roarke agreed. "But Claude's an oil engineer, too. So he does okay."

"Of course, he's not the one having to give birth all those times," Daria said dryly.

"Got a point there." Roarke waved at the man in the plaid shirt, who waved back. "So, what about you?" he asked with studied casualness.

"What about me, what?"

"You and your fiancé ever talk about having kids?"

"Of course." The question stimulated the memory of a conversation. "James says that it's important for a politician to have a family."

"A pretty wife and a couple of cute little kids undoubtedly makes for a better campaign ad," he agreed. "Especially in these days of family values."

He wondered if she knew the rumors Mike had passed on about James Boudreaux having a longtime liaison with a redhead who had worked for a popular

New Orleans escort service before leaving to open her own "modeling agency."

"That's exactly what he said." Her tone was definitely less than enthusiastic.

"Doesn't sound as if you agree," he said mildly.

"I like the idea of children. And I've always wanted a large family. Although not quite as large as your Uncle Claude's," she added hastily. "But I don't believe in using them as political pawns."

"You may have to get over that." He reached over, took hold of her hand and ran his finger over the sparkling diamond ring she was still wearing. "If you intend to be a politician's wife." Roarke knew he'd hurt her when he felt her hand go cold.

"How can you think I could possibly marry James?" she asked quietly. "After last night?"

He hardened his heart against the soft sheen of tears glistening in those wide, wounded eyes.

"Correct me if I'm wrong," he drawled, "but I thought we had an agreement. Last night, as good as it was—as good as you were—was just sex, sugar. No strings, no commitments. We'll enjoy each other until this is over and the bad guys are behind bars. Then we'll move on with our lives."

"That was the agreement, but—"

He cut her off with a curse. "I knew that was a mistake. I knew you couldn't stick to the deal."

"I've never welshed on anything in my life. And if you think I'm going to grovel and beg you to love me, you're going to be waiting until this bayou freezes over." She dropped her feet to the wooden-plank floor of the porch and stood over him, her arms crossed over her breasts.

She was trembling, but the tears threatening in her

eyes had been burned out by lightning flashes of anger. "Last night proved to me that I can't marry James. But just because your oversize ego seems to think that means I want to spend the rest of my life with you, doesn't make it true."

She might actually believe that. But Roarke didn't buy it for a minute. "This has nothing to do with my ego. It's about the fact that just because I spent most of the night inside you, you've started smelling orange blossoms."

"That's not true." All right, perhaps there had been a moment when she'd first come out here this morning, that she'd fantasized about spending the rest of her life here, with Roarke. But at the same time she'd understood that such a scenario was not only impractical, but impossible. "And just because you spent most of the night inside me, doesn't give you the right to treat me like some cheap hooker you picked up in the Quarter."

He dragged his hand through his hair, frustrated by her accusation, but even more frustrated by his own unruly feelings. He'd walked away from countless affairs without looking back, and never had he felt so much as a twinge. Although she insisted she wasn't looking for happily-ever-afters, he felt as if he'd just stomped all over her tender heart.

"If you'd told me in the beginning that you expected pretty words, I would have told you that I was the wrong guy."

"You did tell me you were the wrong man for me," she reminded him.

"Then you should have listened."

"I did listen."

"But you made the decision to sleep with me anyway."

"Because I didn't believe you."

His only response to that was an arched, challenging brow.

Her fingers were itching to slap that smug look off his face, when she suddenly understood.

"I don't know what happened to you in Moscow. But it obviously left emotional scars—"

His booted feet hit the deck. "You don't know what you're talking about." He was on his feet, towering over her, his glare as lethal as any weapon.

"Yes, I do." She also realized that despite her denial about wanting more than he was prepared to offer, she'd fallen in love with this dark and secretive man. "I know that something or someone made you think you can't ever trust again. But you're mistaken, and I also know that deep down inside, you know you're wrong, too, because so far, in the past few days, you've trusted Mike—"

"He's my brother."

"True. But that's not always a given. Surely you've read the story of Cain and Abel."

He shook his head. "Remind me not to argue with a damn lawyer."

Daria ignored that little jibe. "And you've trusted me."

"I didn't have much choice. I told you, I'm after a story, and—"

"And you're a rotten liar." She put her mug down on the railing, closed the scant distance between them and linked her fingers together around his neck. "This isn't about a story." Her body pressed against him—soft, feminine and treacherously alluring. "You do trust me, O'Malley. The same way I trust you. Because we can both deny it until doomsday, but we care. Perhaps more than we should."

There were a hundred—a thousand—reasons why he should cut his losses now and run. While he still could. But the renewed flare of hunger in his loins overruled the voice of reason trying to make itself heard in his head.

He slid his hand between the waistband of the leggings and her smooth silky skin, and cupped her bottom, lifting her against him. Pressing his erection between her legs, he rubbed her back and forth against him in a way that made her moan softly and created an ache somewhere between pain and pleasure.

"The only thing I care about right now is getting laid."

She knew he was being purposefully crude to discourage her. She also knew that Roarke was a far better man than he believed himself to be. And although she had no idea what had happened to so darken his soul, she vowed to stay alive long enough to prove to him that he was a man worthy of love. A man capable of giving love in return.

"All you had to do was ask." She took her hands from around his neck and backed away just enough to allow her to pull the shirt over her head. When her bare breasts beckoned, he bent his head, intending to take one of those sweet rosy tips into his mouth, but she resisted. "Not yet."

She drew the leggings all the way down her legs and pulled them off. She was now down to a pair of scarlet-as-sin panties so skimpy he wondered why she even bothered with them, and a pair of knee-high white socks covered with red hearts.

"Nice socks," he managed.

He wasn't looking at the socks at all, but at the ribbon ties at the sides of her panties. Daria smiled—a slow feminine smile that women have been using to seduce men since the beginning of time.

"It's the season for hearts...Valentine's Day is coming up," she elaborated at his blank look.

"Oh. Yeah." It was more and more difficult to talk around his thickened tongue. After last night he knew her body as well as his own. So why the hell could the sight of it make him feel like a horny, sex-crazed teenager getting his first glimpse of a *Penthouse* magazine?

He leaned back against the railing, watching as she put her left foot up on the chair and slowly rolled the cheery heart-covered sock down her calf with all the erotic skill of a premiere stripper on Bourbon Street.

The second sock joined the first, draped over the back of the wicker chair. When she closed the gap between them and pressed her palm against him, Roarke thought he was going to explode.

Desperate to be inside her again, he ripped the red panties away, then lifted her up, braced her against the wooden railing and entered her fully in one deep, driving thrust. As she closed around him like a hot, tight velvet glove, his release was instantaneous and so explosive that he couldn't think, let alone speak. He simply held her, pinned against the railing, his mouth buried in her neck.

When his mind cooled slightly, he reached between them, found her hard little nub, then adjusted their position so he was pressed against it. He was rewarded by her faint gasp, and felt her literally go weak at the knees in his arms. "Wrap your legs around me, baby," he coaxed, his tongue trailing wetly around her ear. "And hang on."

When Daria did as instructed without question, he began to rotate his hips, massaging her most sensitive flesh, heating it, until he felt her come in a deep, shuddering release.

Although the morning air was cool, they were both drenched in perspiration. It wasn't until he heard the faraway drone of a boat engine that Roarke realized that he'd taken her outside, standing, where anyone could see them. This was the busiest time on the bayou, and although his cabin was more isolated than most, he knew several men—including his uncle—whose crayfish trapping areas were in the vicinity.

"What is it about you?" he murmured as he reached for her sweatshirt, "that makes me lose my head whenever I get within kissing distance?"

"I have no idea." She pulled the sweatshirt over her head, flinching slightly as the fleece slid over nipples that were still ultrasensitive from her earlier sexual hunger. "But when you figure it out, let me know, because I'm the same way around you."

He'd known that, and it gave him more pleasure than it should have. He also knew that women usually found him to be a proficient and satisfying partner. So why should the simple physical act of bringing this particular woman to orgasm make him feel as if he could leap tall buildings in a single bound?

Roarke told himself that nothing had changed. He was still a wanderer. It was in his blood, passed down from father to son. He'd been a loner all of his life, and if there had been a time when he might have contemplated having a normal life, with a wife, some kids and a dog—the kind of life he'd always yearned for as a boy—he'd given up on the idea years ago.

If he had any sense of honor, he would remind Daria that he wasn't the sticking-around type of guy. But when he realized that he'd screwed up again, not only taking her outside in the open, but without additional protection, he found himself imagining her ripe and round with his child. When the idea proved far too appealing, Roarke decided it was past time to leave the cabin and check up on what, if anything, Mike had discovered—about his assailants, Daria's cases and, although he hadn't said anything to Daria, her fiancé.

"I suppose I'd better get going," he said after she'd gotten dressed again and he'd refastened his jeans. Part of him needed to get away from her, to clear his head, to figure out what he was feeling. Another part of him—the terrifying part—seemed more than comfortable just to remain here forever.

"I suppose so." Daria didn't sound any more eager than he was for him to leave. She sighed. "I wish I could remember something else. Since I can recall that man being murdered in the bayou, you'd think being out here would trigger some memory."

"That was the plan." He sat down in the chair next to the one she'd abandoned, and pulled her onto his lap. "But I guess you've been a little distracted."

His hand slipped beneath the sweatshirt to cup her bare breast again, but rather than feeling renewed arousal, she felt utterly comfortable and safe. She laughed as he nuzzled at her ear and tilted her head back, giving his lips access to her throat. "More than a little."

"I don't suppose that the world would come to an end if we had breakfast before I left."

"I think that's a very good idea. After all—" she put her hand against his chest "—you need to keep your strength up."

"Good point." Her smiling lips were too much of a temptation to resist. He touched his mouth to hers. "I'm going to need all the energy I can muster if I'm going to play good guys/bad guys."

She felt his lips curved against hers and knew that he was smiling. She remembered the grim expressions that had seemed normal for him when they'd first met, and realized that the easy enjoyment they seemed able to share together had, for some reason, been a rare thing for him.

"Will you do me one favor before you leave?"

"What?" He was not the kind of man to agree to anything without knowing the terms of the deal. On the other hand, he couldn't think of anything Daria could possibly ask of him that he wouldn't do willingly.

"Will you tell me what happened in Moscow?"

She felt him go absolutely still. His body tensed and she thought he'd stopped breathing. Indeed, although her hand was pressed against his chest, she could have sworn that even his heart had ceased to beat.

Dammit, anyway. She'd come up with the one request that was going to prove not only difficult, but downright painful. Although he knew Natasha's death hadn't really been his fault—she had, it seemed, been more than willing to kill him—guilt still nagged at him, weighing heavily on his shoulders.

"It's standing between us," she said softly, but insistently. "*She's* standing between us. And although I realize that we have an agreement that this is strictly sex, I've never been all that kinky."

A warning flashed in his eyes. "What does that mean?"

Reminding herself that in the outside world she was a competent, intelligent trial lawyer, capable of surviving a great deal more than a masculine glare, Daria ignored it.

"It means," she said, "I'm not really into three-somes."

At first Roarke didn't understand. "You think I am?"

"She's between us, Roarke." Daria cupped his face between her palms, her expression more earnest than he'd ever seen it. "She has been from the beginning."

"Not while we're making—" it was his turn to quickly catch himself "—not while we're in bed," he alleged.

"No. Not there."

Those were the only times he'd allowed his emotions to slip the tight rein he kept them on; the rare instances when he would allow her a glimpse of his inner self. Beneath the cold, forbidding exterior was a warm, caring, compassionate man. Who was also the most passionate and demanding lover she'd ever known. Yet because he gave of himself so freely, Daria never felt as if he asked more of her than she was capable, or willing, to give.

He exhaled a long breath. "You're not going to drop this, are you?"

"I'm sorry. I don't think I can."

He sighed again and rested his cheek atop her head. Utilizing more patience than she sensed was usual for her, she managed to remain quiet and not push while he battled what she suspected were his own inner demons.

"I suppose, if you really feel as if Natasha's ghost is hovering somewhere between us, I owe you the truth. As grim as it is."

Her rival had a name. *Natasha*. And, unless Roarke was speaking figuratively—which, from his bleak tone and even bleaker expression, she didn't think he was—the woman was dead.

Knowing that people tended to dwell only on the positive attributes of those they'd loved, then lost, she wondered how she was supposed to live up to remembered perfection. His next words proved exactly how mistaken she could be.

"Natasha was the most self-serving, amoral woman I've ever met. And, although I know I should be sorry she's dead, I really can't be. Because if it hadn't been her, it would have been me." And if he'd been killed, he would never have met Daria. Never experienced how special sex between two people who felt strongly about one another could be.

"Was her death an accident?"

"Hardly."

Please, Daria begged silently, *don't tell me you killed her.*

"The only accident was that *she* died. Instead of me." All the passionate fire she was accustomed to seeing in his dark blue eyes had vanished, like a candle snuffed out by an icy wind. "The irony is that she'd been the one to set up the assassination in the first place. Unfortunately, she made the mistake of trusting her own people. The same way I'd made the mistake of trusting her."

Without even knowing the details, Daria understood the reason Roarke hadn't been able to lift his guard with her. Except, of course, as he'd already pointed out, when they were making love. He might call it having sex, but impossible as it seemed on such short acquaintance, she, at least, had been making love.

"I don't suppose it would do any good to tell you that you can trust me?"

The tension was strung like an electric wire between them. Her tone was soft and hesitant. And even as he found himself wanting to assure her that he would believe any story she told him, he forced himself to keep a cool head.

"No offense, baby." The remote tone, along with the snort of derision, was planned. The stiletto-sharp edge of sarcasm was not. "But I've heard those pretty words before."

He knew he'd hurt her. With his arms wrapped around her, he was aware when she flinched. He half expected feminine weeping. Or anger. Instead, she stood and met his mocking look levelly, her expression calm. Almost, he thought with surprise, serene.

"If your story's true—"

"It is."

"Then I can certainly understand how you'd be horribly disillusioned. But I'm not Natasha, whoever and whatever she was." Now that she'd come this far, Daria decided to go for broke. "And what's happening between us—whether we like it or not—does not resemble, in any way, what the two of you shared."

Not willing to give her the upper hand, he twisted his lips in a parody of a smile, reached out and ran his hand up her thigh. "Want to bet?"

Daria had tried enough courtroom cases to have developed some acting ability. At least enough to be able to maintain her dignity under his mocking gaze.

"I already have."

That stated, she turned and walked back into the cabin, leaving Roarke frustrated and unable to decide whether to curse or laugh at the impossibility of the situation he'd gotten himself into.

12

ROARKE REALIZED THAT there was an outside chance that whoever was after Daria might manage to catch up with him at the bait shop. And this time, he knew, they might actually kill him, just for pissing them off by getting away the first time.

Just as he hadn't wanted to die without taking Daria to bed, neither did he want to go out with her believing that he compared her, in any way, to Natasha.

Pushing himself out of the chair, he went back into the cabin where Daria was mixing eggs with a fork in a white earthenware bowl.

"It's me you're mad at," he said. "No point in taking it out on the eggs."

She didn't look up at him. Nor did she pause in her energetic beating. "I thought I'd make an omelet. Amazingly, your uncle Claude stocked the refrigerator with cheese and mushrooms and green onions, and, of course, Tabasco sauce."

"Can't leave out the hot pepper," he agreed. Since she'd turned her back, she missed his conciliatory smile. "And it's not that amazing he stocked the larder well. Among Cajuns, cooking tends to be considered men's work. In fact, cooking your first gumbo while the other guys are playing bouré—that's a card game—is kinda like a rite of passage."

"How fascinating." Her tone said otherwise. Still

refusing to look at him, she put a pat of butter into an iron skillet.

He knew he deserved the silent treatment, but didn't want to leave with things unsettled. "I never would have guessed you to be the type of female to hold a grudge."

She sighed, put the bowl on the scarred wooden counter and turned around. "I don't think I am." She gave another sigh, more weary than the first. "In fact, I know I'm not. I couldn't do my job if I wasn't able to let go of things."

"That's work. This is different."

"Yes." She was biting her bottom lip again in a way that he suspected she would never do in court, and that made him want to kiss away the pain caused by his unnecessarily cruel words.

The butter in the pan Roarke usually used to fry catfish in began to sizzle. Reaching around her, he pulled it off the burner and turned off the range.

"We can eat later. Right now we need to talk. About Moscow, and Natasha, and most of all, about us."

At least he was willing to admit there was an *us*. Daria decided that was progress, of sorts.

Although she didn't respond, neither did she resist when he took her hand, linked their fingers together and led her back out onto the porch.

Daria didn't know what she'd expected him to say, but she hadn't expected him to share his life story. When he began telling her about his childhood, growing up with Mike and Shayne and their mother, she suspected it was not a story he had told often. Since she'd already admitted to herself how much she cared for this man, Daria allowed hope to flutter fledgling wings in her heart.

"Of course, Mom had a big family to fill in for our dad," he told her. "But it really wasn't the same."

"No." Daria sighed, thinking of all the years she'd spent alone in private schools while her parents traveled the globe. "But at least you had your mother."

"Yeah." Roarke's smile was quick, uncensored and warm. "She's a cool lady. You'll like her. And I know she'll like you."

Daria had to ask. "So I'm going to meet her?"

"If she wasn't in New Iberia, visiting her sister, I doubt I could have kept her away this long. Especially since by now Mike will have told her that her middle son has himself a lady friend."

"I have a hard time believing that's so unusual," she murmured. After all, a man didn't reach the level of competition in lovemaking this man had without considerable practice.

"You're different. Mike spotted that right off the bat."

Again, hope flared. Still cautious, Daria managed to bank it. "I suppose that's because he's a detective."

Roarke laughed at that, a rich, booming sound she knew would always have the power to warm her. "Got a point there," he said easily. "Mike was a great cop. He'll also make some woman a terrific husband."

"So you've said. And it's a good try, but you're not going to pass me on to your brother when you're done with me, Roarke. Because I won't go along with the idea. And I suspect Michael wouldn't, either."

Roarke wondered what would happen if he just flat out told her that he wasn't certain he was ever going to be done with her. Since the idea was too new to share, he kept it to himself. For now.

"I just wanted to warn you—"

"Consider me warned. And have you O'Malley brothers ever considered that perhaps your mother didn't feel her life was such a loss? That the times she shared with your father were worth all those years he was away chasing his dream?"

"I never thought of it that way," Roarke admitted. And he knew damn well Mike hadn't. Of the three of them, Mike hated his father the most for having essentially deserted the family.

"That's because you're a man."

"What about you?" he asked, genuinely curious. "Would you put up with a husband who only showed up unexpectedly, without warning, every few months? Or even years?"

"No." This time she didn't surprise him. Her answer was exactly what he'd suspected she would say. What he'd feared. "When I get married, it's going to be to a man who's willing to commit to an equal partnership. And I don't see how he could do that if he wasn't ever home."

Neither could Roarke. Which was, he reminded himself, his dilemma. If he was considering a life with Daria. Which he wasn't, he assured himself.

The hell he wasn't.

"You could always travel with him."

"I don't like war. I don't like reading about it in the newspaper, I don't like seeing it on television and I don't have to travel to a war zone to know that I wouldn't like it in person."

"No one does."

She gave him a long look. "Yet you've built a career on exactly that."

"True. And did you ever think that perhaps I'm getting a little tired of watching innocent people die because a few greedy people in the world can't figure out a way to get along without bloodshed?"

"If that's the case, perhaps you ought to rethink your career choice." Her mild tone belied the sudden hammering of her heart.

"Now that you bring it up, that's precisely what I returned home to do." He saw the reluctant hope shining in her remarkable gold eyes, knew he'd been the one to put it there, and this time found himself unable to dash it. "I was ready to quit the network—"

"You were going to quit? Why?"

"I figured it was either that or get canned. After I got a little carried away and practically killed the guy responsible for the car bomb that killed Natasha. With my bare hands."

The network brass had been right, Roarke realized reluctantly. He *had* gone over the edge. Obviously, spending all those years documenting the worst deeds that human beings were willing to do to one another had deadened some of his humane instincts.

She looked down at the hand that still held hers, tried to imagine it capable of such violence and couldn't. "That's a little hard to picture."

He shrugged. "You had to have been there, I guess.... Natasha was the mistress of one of Russia's top mob bosses. I was sitting in the bar of my hotel one day when she came up to me and promised me the inside scoop on how the mob worked. She also said she was afraid her lover was trying to kill her."

The significance of that meeting hit home. "No wonder you didn't trust me," Daria murmured.

"The circumstances were eerily similar."

"It must be incredibly difficult playing the role of a

knight in shining armor, rescuing damsels in distress."

Personally, Roarke had always figured if he had lived back in the days when knights rode off to battle in armor, his would definitely have been more than a little tarnished.

"But you got involved with me anyway," Daria said softly. "For the story."

"No." He shook his head and met her questioning gaze straight on. "I've been trying to tell myself that from the beginning. That all you meant to me was a story. But I was wrong. And as for that knight-in-shining-armor stuff, it wasn't because I felt any chivalrous instinct to protect a damsel in distress. Because believe me, sweetheart, after Moscow, that was the last thing on my mind."

He cupped her cheek with his free hand. "Do you believe in fate? Or destiny?"

"I don't think so."

"Neither did I. But I've spent the past two months trying to figure out what went wrong in Moscow. How I could have made such a fatal error in judgment when I've always prided myself on my instincts.

"Now I realize that everything that went wrong in Moscow was predestined to happen so I'd end up here, back home in New Orleans, at this time, with you."

Daria was amazed by this direct assertion. And after that declaration, she decided it was time to be equally as honest.

"I suppose this is where I admit that I've had a crush on you for years."

"You're kidding."

He'd heard that from other women before. But they

tended to be news groupies, women who hung out in the bars at hotels where the press tended to gather, the same way other women gravitated toward sports bars hoping to meet—and sleep with—athletes. In his younger years, Roarke had enjoyed taking advantage of what they offered; these days, although still no candidate for sainthood, he was a great deal choosier.

"You don't have to look so surprised." A pretty shade of pink tinged her cheeks. "You're very good at what you do. And, of course, you always looked so dashing in those shirts with the epaulets."

"Any guy can buy them at Banana Republic."

"Ah, but not every man can wear them with such panache." Her grin was quick and bright. "I suppose, when I first saw you in the Blue Bayou, I confused your television image with the man."

So had all those groupies who'd been so eager to go to bed with him. "And now?"

"I realize that the real man is even better than the TV newscaster." All those other women could eat their hearts out, Daria decided. Because whether he realized it or not, she was going to keep Roarke.

"That's exactly what you're supposed to say, sweetheart."

He kissed her again—another long, heartfelt kiss that spoke volumes and promised the future he was not yet fully prepared to offer. "Of course, I'm not certain you've proved a real good judge of men."

She drew her head back. "We're back to James, aren't we?"

"The guy's a jerk, Daria. He was the class bully as a kid and now that he's gotten some power, he's probably even worse. I can't understand how an intelligent woman like you got mixed up with him in the first place."

"He used to be a prosecutor."

"So?"

"So it was nice to have someone to talk about my work with."

"Hell, I like talking shop with female reporters, but I've never felt the urge to marry one of them."

"I don't know how I got engaged," she admitted. "He was home one weekend about six months ago, we went out to dinner, and suddenly he produced a ring. Since I didn't know what to say—"

"How about *no?*"

She sighed. "I did, at first. But James can be very persuasive. He put forth a very logical argument about why we'd make a perfect team."

"I'm not certain that falling in love and getting married has much to do with logic."

"You're probably right."

"Did you love him?"

Daria looked up at him curiously. "Why should you care?"

Roarke shrugged. He'd been asking himself the same question and hadn't liked the answers he'd been coming up with. "I told you, the guy's a jerk and a bully. I don't like the idea of you being under his thumb."

"Believe me, Roarke," she said firmly, "I've no intention of being under any man's thumb."

Deciding the conversation had wandered too deeply into the personal again, Roarke turned it back to the little matter of their puzzle.

"I really should be going soon." His lips returned to pluck at hers.

"You really should have breakfast," she murmured, sinking into the kiss.

He was hungry. But not for any omelet. "I've got a better idea." He stood and scooped her into his arms and carried her back to the soft wide bed.

Their lovemaking was sweeter than ever. They seemed to have moved to a level in their relationship where they could enjoy each other with a lingering pleasure born of the commitment neither had yet spoken out loud.

There would be time for pretty speeches later, Roarke decided as he followed Daria into the mists. Because the one thing he was sure of was that nothing—and no one—was going to keep them from having a future together.

SHE WAS SO LOVELY. So sweet. Roarke looked down at Daria, sleeping lightly, imagined spending the rest of his life waking up next to this woman and wondered how he'd gotten so damn lucky. He felt so good he almost laughed out loud. But as much as he wished he could keep her hidden away out here in the bayou forever, the fact remained that they couldn't get on with their lives until her would-be assassins were safely behind bars. A random, highly impractical thought flashed through his mind: the idea of escaping with her now to some far-distant land, changing their names and living incognito among the natives. But, even if they could pull off such a ruse, he knew it wasn't fair. Not to Daria, or to his family.

There might have been a time when that wouldn't have seemed so important. But since returning to Louisiana, Roarke had come to appreciate exactly how much family meant to him. Although the idea of getting any woman pregnant had always been anathema to Roarke, he grinned as he thought ahead to the distant day when he would be able to tell Mary O'Malley that he and Daria were about to make her a grandmother.

The idea continued to please him as he slipped silently out of bed, gathered up his clothes and dressed on the porch to avoid waking her. She needed her sleep. He would leave a note, he decided, not wanting to admit, even to himself, that he wasn't willing to say goodbye. Even for such a brief time as it would take to go to the bait shop and see what messages Mike might have for him.

Roarke wrote the note on the back of a scrap of envelope, then poled the boat away from the cabin, only starting the engine when he was far enough away that he didn't think the sound would wake her. As he headed back through the waters he knew like the back of his hand, Roarke forced warm thoughts of Daria from his mind and concentrated on the mission of saving her life.

DARIA WAS DISAPPOINTED, but not surprised when she awoke to find Roarke gone. She'd known he was headed off to that bait shop to learn what, if anything, Michael had discovered. She also wished he'd wakened her. If anything should happen to him without her having a chance to tell him that she loved him...

No! She shook her head, refusing to even consider such a horrendous thought. Roarke would be all right. She couldn't allow herself to think otherwise.

She pulled on her leggings, sweatshirt and sneakers, and went back into the kitchen, dumped out the beaten eggs that were still sitting in a bowl on the counter waiting to be made into omelets, and settled for toast and coffee.

Nervous as a cat, she paced the cabin waiting for Roarke's return. She wished she'd gone with him. She should have gone with him. After all, he was only involved in this because of her. And what if Michael wanted to ask her a question? How could she be of any help all the way out here in the middle of nowhere?

"Dammit, Roarke," she muttered, "when you get back we're going to have to have a long talk about equality in a relationship." She knew he was only trying to keep her safe, but Daria welcomed her irritation. It kept her mind occupied—almost but not quite preventing her from worrying.

She skimmed through a stack of magazines and noticed with disinterest that they all seemed to have to do with either fishing or hunting. Beneath the magazines she found a leather sheath holding the ugliest knife she'd ever seen. And, unfortunately, in her business she'd seen quite a few. As she put it back down, a memory flashed—a memory of a similar knife being held against a man's throat as a rope was tied around his neck.

Her blood chilled, her knees threatened to buckle. She lowered herself to a straight-backed wooden chair, and although her first instinct was to shut her mind to the scene, Daria knew that it would provide her with an important clue.

She could see them as she'd remembered them before, in the bayou. A group of men holding torches and wearing executioner's hoods, were standing in a circle. In the middle of the circle, a terrified young man begged for mercy.

"You had your mercy," a deep, all-too-familiar voice said. "Handed down by what is laughingly referred to as the justice system. And now you're going to have your punishment."

He tugged the end of the rope, which was looped around the limb of a cypress tree. The prisoner's feet lifted off the ground.

"You'll never get away with this," the young man sobbed. "Please, if you just let me go, I'll never tell anyone. I'll leave the city. The state. I'll go to—"

"The only place you're going to is hell." That said, the man backed away.

A moment later another hooded man lifted a shotgun to his shoulder. Daria could hear the sound of the gun being cocked even over the prisoner's continued entreaties. His eyes, in the flickering torchlight, were wide and terrified. And then something happened. A new expression came over his face and he looked as cold and evil as the men who were about to kill him.

"I may be going to hell, but you'll end up there, too," he threatened.

"That may be," the voice she recognized answered in a pleasant tone that was in direct contrast to the horror of the scene. "But you'll get there first."

He made a slight motion with his hand. An instant later, the sound of the shotgun reverberated through the bayou like the roar of cannon fire. A hole the size of a man's fist opened up in the prisoner's chest; his dying heart pumped blood onto the ground like a geyser.

The men stood silently, watching as the moist earth soaked up their prisoner's life force. When his legs had stopped jerking and his blood had stopped pumping, they cut him down and tossed him into the bayou with a splash.

When they pulled off their hoods, Daria watched in mind-numbing shock as each of the men—men she knew personally, policemen and judges she worked with every day—shook the hand of their leader, James Boudreaux.

"Oh, my God." She lowered her aching head to her hands and began to weep as she'd not been able to do that night.

It all flooded back. The six-month investigation that had led her into the bayou that night. The suspicion she hadn't dared share with anyone—including the man she'd been engaged to marry. *Especially* the man she'd been engaged to marry.

She raised her head and looked down at the diamond ring that glittered mockingly on her left hand. She'd always prided herself on being able to read human nature. But the one time it had really mattered, she'd obviously made a fatal mistake.

She pushed herself to her feet and resumed pacing, more edgy than ever. She needed to tell Roarke what she remembered. But how?

"Dammit!" She went out onto the porch and looked out over the miles of empty bayou. There was no way to reach him. She had no choice. She would have to wait until he returned. And hope that it wouldn't be too late.

THE BAIT SHOP was typical for the area—constructed of cypress, tin-roofed, with a boat dock, scales for weighing the daily catch, crayfish traps and tanks stocked with minnows for bait. A handmade sign above the door instructed fishermen that if they sold their fish there, they were expected to buy their cheese—also used for bait—there, as well.

Knowing that to appear rushed was considered the height of rudeness in this part of the country, Roarke forced himself to pass the time of day with the group of men sitting around on the dock who were eating barbecue and drinking beer, discussing the weather, the fishing, the success or failure of the hunting and trapping, and, as always, those damn oil companies that had brought some wealth to the bayou, but even more environmental danger.

"One of these days, life as we know it will be gone," one of the old-timers predicted. "The oil bust was bad enough. Now all these alligator and crayfish farms sure aren't helping. If people keep leavin' it's gonna be like another Great Exile."

"I'd be like a sick dog if I had to leave here," another man said.

The others murmured agreement. No one asked Roarke what he'd been doing during his time away in the outside world. Life among what some of the old-timers still called "the Americans," did not interest them. This was the real world. The only one that counted. And although he understood their parochialism, Roarke feared he was looking at an endangered species.

After promising not to be a stranger, he went into the office and hooked his laptop up to the phone on the rickety old pine desk.

Mike had obviously come through. But along with the files was another E-mail message to call immediately.

"What the hell took you so long?" Mike answered, back in New Orleans.

"I got a little sidetracked."

"That figures. How is Daria, anyway?"

"She's fine. And safe." And Roarke had every intention of keeping her that way.

"That remains to be seen. We found what those cops were looking for."

"What? And how?"

"Sugar went into the projects. Heard there was a kid there who likes to mug folks foolish enough to visit Marie Laveau's tomb. He was run off by your lady friend's would-be killer. But he came back the next morning to pick up any spare change that might be lying around the tomb and found a computer diskette."

"What was on it?"

"A list of cases the prosecutor's office had lost in the last six months."

"So? That'd be a matter of public record."

"This was a rather unique list," Mike said. "All the acquitted were men. And all of them mysteriously left the parish shortly after juries found them innocent."

"I don't suppose it'd be unusual to want to get a new start." Even as he said it, Roarke knew he was grasping at straws. The truth was, homegrown criminals rarely left the place where they felt safe. Where they had a support system.

"There's always an outside possibility," Mike allowed. "But we're talking about six men. In six months."

Roarke whistled softly.

"That's not all," Mike said. "Turns out that they all seemed to disappear on weekends that Congressman Boudreaux returned home to Louisiana to visit his constituents."

And his fiancée.

"Hell." Roarke dragged his hand through his hair. "Sounds like what we've got going is a rogue vengeance group."

"Sounds like it. You know, there were rumors of something called the Tribunal back when I was on the force. But I never really believed them. And no one ever would have invited me to join." Mike paused. "It gets worse."

"What?" As if things weren't already bad enough. Roarke felt a fist twisting his gut.

"Boudreaux flew into town this morning. He took off a little while ago in a police helicopter headed out into the bayou."

A thought suddenly occurred to Roarke. A realization that there was a good chance James Boudreaux might be able to locate the cabin. The bayou had changed considerably over the years since they'd been boys together; most of the twisting, narrow old watercourses had been straightened and channelized by the Corps of Engineers. But from the air...

"I think it's time to send in the cavalry." With that, Roarke hung up the phone, turned off the computer and left the office.

"Gotta go," he told the owner of the shop. He tossed a twenty on the counter. "This should pay for the phone call. And a round of beer for the guys."

He ran down the dock to the boat, untied it, and took off with a roar of the engine.

With one eye on the darkening sky, he headed back into the swamp toward his cabin, and although it had been a very long time since he'd ventured inside a church, Roarke found himself praying that he wouldn't be too late.

13

DARIA HEARD THE DISTANT sound over the still, dark water. At first she thought it was a boat engine. Perhaps Roarke's Uncle Claude was returning from checking his traps. He could take her to Roarke. Or, even better yet, perhaps it was Roarke himself, back with news from Michael. Not that it was necessary, now that she remembered everything.

Including the horrifying knowledge that the place where the vigilantes murdered their victims just happened to be an alligator farm, which conveniently took care of the bodies.

The thought made her shudder. She stood and leaned over the railing, looking in the direction of the droning mechanical sound that was coming closer.

And then she saw it—the helicopter approaching like a huge bird of prey from behind a dark gray cloud. When she recognized it as a police copter, Daria's heart trebled its beat and her mind leaped into overdrive.

"There has to be some way out of this," she assured herself firmly.

She was, after all, an intelligent woman, with an unprecedented conviction rate. If she hadn't succeeded in sending so many criminals to jail, a lot more bodies would have been turned into gator food. Even as her mind raced, she wondered if any of those angry men she'd sent to prison realized exactly how lucky they were.

She ran back into the house as the copter hovered nearby, the pilot obviously seeking out a landing place.

"What kind of hunting cabin is this?" she yelled in frustration when she found not a single shotgun, rifle or handgun anywhere.

She heard the sound of the rotors slicing the air as the helicopter came closer and closer to the ground. And then, nothing. Only a deathly silence.

In desperation, knowing that a knife would be no real defense against the weapons the rogue cops would undoubtedly be carrying, Daria grabbed the leather-sheathed knife, stuck it into the waistband of her leggings and pulled her sweatshirt down over it.

Then, deciding nothing would be gained by trying to hide inside, when they'd already undoubtedly seen her, she went back out onto the porch. And waited.

When she viewed the familiar face of the man walking toward her, Daria did not have to feign surprise. "James! What are you doing here?"

His smile was bright and friendly, the same one he used during campaign appearances to woo constituents. The same one he'd once used to convince her to marry him.

"That should be obvious, of course. I'm looking for you. I've heard the most distressing news concerning you lately, darling."

"Really? What news is that?"

"I really don't know where to begin." He was climbing the stairs and for a quick, fleeting moment she considered pushing him back down and running away. But the sky was growing darker again—she could taste another Gulf storm brewing in the air—and the idea of getting lost in the dark out here in the middle of this vast swampland was even more terrifying than anything this man might do.

"If it's about Roarke O'Malley, I can explain—"

"You don't have to explain anything. Roarke and I are old friends."

"Really?" That certainly wasn't how Roarke had described it.

"Of course. How do you think I knew about this place? We used to spend a lot of time here when we were kids. Fishing, hunting bullfrogs." He was on the porch now, only a few feet away, when he paused and glanced around. "Once we got into high school, the O'Malley brothers started bringing girls out here." His cold flat gaze reminded her of a reptile as it flicked over her. "I see not much has changed."

"I'm sorry." That was an understatement. Daria was truly sorry she'd gotten involved with a murderer. Even sorrier yet that she still hadn't figured a way to survive whatever horrendous fate James undoubtedly had planned for her. "I suppose it wouldn't matter if I told you that it was just a fling, that I'd met him in a bar, and—"

He slapped her face hard.

"I never would have taken you for a slut, darling." Her blood, which was already chilled, turned to ice. His tone was the same pleasant one he'd used just before he'd killed that neighborhood drug dealer. "In fact, if I'd known you were the type of woman who slept with any man who propositioned her, I never would have proposed."

His smile, a cold slash of white teeth, did not reach his eyes. "As an elected representative of the people of

Louisiana, I have an obligation to marry a suitable woman." His fingertips trailed over the skin his palm had reddened. "Obviously, that isn't you."

"Obviously." She pulled the ring off her finger and held it out to him. "You're right, I don't deserve—"

Another slap, this time to her other cheek, cut her off again in mid-sentence and caused her to drop the ring. "We've been playing games long enough. Where is it?"

"What?"

He struck her again, this time hard enough to make her see stars. "The diskette. Where the hell is the diskette?"

"I don't know. It's the truth!" she cried out, this time lifting her arms to ward off his hand, which had curled into a tight fist. "I had it at the hotel, when I discovered Martin dead. But then your hired police thug dragged me through the park into the cemetery and my purse came open, and when I woke up in the hospital, it was gone."

His eyes narrowed. "If you're lying—"

"I'm not."

He gave her another long, probing look, then shrugged. "It doesn't matter. The diskette doesn't prove a thing. It only makes for intriguing conjecture. Without you to testify to what you saw in the bayou—"

"I didn't see anything," she said quickly.

Too quickly, she realized as she watched the satisfied expression replace the frustration on his handsome face. Dammit! It had only been a guess. And she'd blown it. Big time.

"I don't suppose you'd believe that I'd keep quiet about this."

"You? Ms. Dudley Do-Right?" He laughed at the notion. "Not for a minute."

Daria opted for a different tack. "Why, James?" she asked quietly. "With all you have going for you, with all the success you've achieved, why would you risk everything to kill those men?"

"They weren't men, darling. They were trash. Lower than trash, they were scum. After the heinous crimes they committed, they deserved the death penalty." His matter-of-fact tone revealed not an iota of remorse.

"But juries found them not guilty."

His answer was a ripe, vicious curse. "If you and your colleagues had done your job, they never would have been released into decent society. But you and those other incompetent prosecutors failed, Daria. So we had to do your work for you."

"We being the Tribunal." She'd recalled all the details she'd uncovered about the group of rogue cops and judges while waiting for Roarke to return.

"You're a clever girl, Daria. Too bad it's going to cost you your life."

"Speaking of killing, why did you murder Martin? He didn't even know any details of the case."

"We had no way of knowing what you'd told him. And, unfortunately, one of the men got a bit over-eager."

"You'll never get away with it, you know." Her calm voice belied her screaming nerves. "Roarke knows everything—"

"Your lover will be dead before nightfall. And his brother, too."

She closed her eyes briefly, too pained for words at the thought of the death of the two men who'd risked their lives for a woman they'd not even known four days ago.

"Please, James, if you don't kill Roarke—"

"Oh, believe me, darling, I will. In fact, I intend to take care of both brothers personally. The O'Malleys have been a pain in the ass for years. Even before Roarke decided to sleep with my fiancée. It'll be a pleasure to watch them beg for mercy."

"They'd never beg."

He ran the back of his hand down her cheek in a parody of a caress. "Believe me, Daria, after a few hours, they'll be begging me to put them out of their misery."

His fingers trailed around her jaw, down her throat and slipped beneath the neck of her sweatshirt. "You know," he murmured, "perhaps you'd like to watch. After I take you to bed, one last time."

Daria vowed not to let this man—this killer!—put a single hand on her body ever again. Since it seemed she truly was going to die, she would rather go down fighting and was desperately wondering how she could best use the knife when a crackling sound distracted her.

"Damn." James plucked a walkie-talkie she hadn't noticed earlier from his belt. "What the hell is it?"

"There's a storm front moving in fast from the Gulf," the disembodied voice said over the static. "If we don't leave right now, we may get stuck out here."

James cursed. His reptilian eyes moved slowly over Daria again. "I suppose we'll have time for fun and games later," he mused. "In fact, now that I think about it, perhaps, after I'm finished with you, I'll hand you over to the other Tribunal members. As a reward for work well-done."

Daria would use the knife on herself before she permitted anything like that to happen. But there was still time, she reminded herself. As long as she managed to remain alive, there was hope for escape.

He pulled a pistol from a shoulder holster beneath his jacket and pointed it at her. "You heard the man. Let's get going."

Having no choice, Daria walked down the stairs, fearing that once she got into that helicopter, Roarke would never be able to find her.

She was on her own.

As she climbed aboard the helicopter, Daria recognized the cop immediately. "It's you!"

The man who'd nearly killed her in the cemetery had the gall to grin. "Fancy meeting you again." The leer in his eyes gave her an idea.

"Isn't it a small world," she murmured. "Perhaps, now that the three of us are here together, you can tell James what you really think of him."

"What's she talking about?" James's glance went from Daria to the pilot, who shrugged.

"Who knows? She's a woman. They all lie." He started the engine; the copter rose from the patch of solid ground he'd found amid the swamp and took off. Daria's heart sank as she watched Roarke's cabin rapidly get smaller and smaller.

"He doesn't think you're much of a man," Daria said conversationally. "In fact, I believe he suggested that you were a pansy." She glanced over at the pilot. "Wasn't that the word you used?"

He shot her a quelling glare. "Bitch."

"This is all very illuminating," James said smoothly. "But it isn't going to work, Daria."

"What isn't going to work?"

"Getting the two of us to argue over you. In the first place, you're not worth it." It was his turn to glance over at the pilot. "She's frigid. The entire time we were together, I don't recall her having a single orgasm."

"You know what they say," Daria retorted as thunder rumbled over the sound of the rotors spinning overhead. Lightning flashed on the horizon and rain began pounding on the convex windshield. "There's no such thing as a frigid woman. Just bad lovers. Which was pretty much what your friend here assured me."

"You told me you were a virgin," the pilot grumbled.

"That wasn't really a lie," Daria said. "Since James has admitted that what I told you was mostly true. He never did make a real woman out of me." She sighed. "In truth, I don't think he had it in him."

She turned back to her former fiancé. "Roarke does," she continued in a conversational tone that suggested they were discussing nothing more personal than the weather, which was growing uglier by the minute. "I couldn't begin to count the number of times he made me come in a single night. Why—" her voice dropped to its lower registers "—he even made me scream."

As she'd hoped it would, her assertion caused jealousy to flare. A dark red flush rose from his collar, suffusing his face. "I'll make you scream."

He dragged her against him, thrust one hand beneath her sweatshirt and squeezed her breast in a way designed to bring pain rather than pleasure. The other hand moved to her waistband, intent on yanking down her leggings.

When she bucked against his intimate touch, he

stumbled against the pilot, who cursed again. "If you're going to rape the chick, can you at least wait until I get this bird on the ground? Because if you keep this up, you'll get us all killed."

James turned to watch as the man steadied the bucking helicopter. "Just keep your mind on your flying," he snarled. "And later, when I've got her warmed up, I may even let you have the opportunity to prove your overstated claims of sexual prowess."

It was the chance Daria had been hoping for. She yanked the knife from its sheath beneath her shirt and lunged toward his back. At the last second James began to turn away from the pilot and the knife slashed into his shoulder, instead.

Roaring with pain and fury, he threw her away from him. Daria landed heavily against the pilot. Shouting and cursing, he struggled to regain control of the copter that had suddenly begun to spin downward in dizzying circles.

She had no idea how long it took for the helicopter to fall out of the sky. It seemed like an eternity of spinning and rolling and shouting. She lost her balance and all sense of which way was up or down. Black spots flashed in front of her eyes. And then they hit the water with a bone-rattling shock. Everything went deathly still.

It took a moment for Daria to realize she was still alive. Another moment to realize that both men had been knocked out and to recognize the smell of gasoline. Even though he'd had every intention of killing her, Daria felt horrible about standing on top of James's unconscious body in order to reach the helicopter door over her head. At first it wouldn't budge. She tried again, harder. And again.

Screaming with frustration, she tried it once more. This time the door moved and she was able to push it open far enough to pull herself up and out of the cockpit.

Half running, half swimming, she splashed through the swampy water, struggling to reach solid ground as the driving cold rain pounded down on her like bullets. She'd just managed to crawl onto a spot of high marshy ground and was on her knees, bent over at the waist, gasping and coughing, when there was a sound like a thousand claps of thunder going off all at once.

She looked up just in time to see the helicopter go up in a blinding fireball that shook the bayou and felt like a furnace against her skin. And then everything went black.

ROARKE WAS RACING across the water, headed back to the cabin, terrified he would be too late, when he heard the unmistakable sound of a helicopter. He watched it rise above the trees and head away from the cabin and hoped that they'd taken Daria hostage, rather than killing her on the spot. Afraid Mike wouldn't manage to get backup here in time, he cursed, and was trying to decide his next move when what he saw caused his heart to lodge in his throat.

The copter was going down.

"No!" Roarke watched, horrified, as the helicopter hit the water. Screamed when he saw it explode. Daria couldn't be in there, he told himself. Experience had taught him that life was anything but fair. But he refused to believe that the fates, or God, or whatever forces were controlling his life, would be cruel enough to force him to watch two lovers die in explosions.

Watching Natasha die had made him want to quit his job.

If Daria had been in that copter when it had blown sky-high, Roarke knew he wouldn't want to keep on living.

DARIA WAS LYING on the cold wet ground. Although she'd regained consciousness, she was still dazed. And more than a little shaken. She was trying to focus her befogged, muddled mind when she thought she heard a familiar sound over the rain and thunder.

"It's not him," she warned herself. "You're obviously delirious. He wouldn't even know how to find you."

But as her mind cleared, she realized that the fire that was beginning to die down would undoubtedly attract somebody.

Perhaps it wasn't Roarke at all. Perhaps it was merely a trapper who'd seen the explosion and was coming here out of curiosity. That would be good enough.

"Anything to keep from spending the night out here," she said with a shudder.

The sound grew closer. And closer still. Daria managed to push herself to her knees again and looked out through the slanting curtain of icy rain. Watching. Waiting.

And then she saw him—pulling the mud boat out of the water and running toward her. She tried once again to stand, but her legs wouldn't hold her. So, with the rain and tears of joy streaming down her face, she began crawling toward him.

His heart was pounding so hard and so fast, Roarke could have sworn he was having a heart attack. His own legs none too steady, when he reached her he dropped to his knees and gathered her into his arms. He kissed her—her lips, her blistered face, her temples, her eyelids—tasting the salt of tears, not knowing if they belonged to Daria or to him.

He was a man who'd always made his living with words. As he'd piloted the boat through the bayou, he'd thought of all the things he wanted to say to Daria. All the things he needed to say to her. All the promises he intended to make.

But there would be time for all that later. A lifetime, he thought with uncharacteristic wonder.

He tenderly framed her face between his palms. "You're going to marry me."

Daria was laughing and crying all at the same time. "Is that a proposal?"

"Didn't it sound like one?"

"It sounded like an order." A wonderful, glorious, heavenly order.

"Lord, that's what I get for falling in love with a lawyer," he grumbled. "Would you just say yes, dammit?"

He loved her! Not only that, he'd said those all-important words out loud. And although she'd been prepared to wait for them—for as long as it took—the pleasure of hearing them warmed her to the core, making her suddenly oblivious to the rain, the cold, the horror she'd experienced.

"Yes, dammit." As she watched his obvious relief, Daria laughed. Then lifted her face for Roarke's kiss.

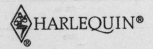

Take 4 bestselling love stories FREE

Plus get a FREE surprise gift!

Special Limited-time Offer

Mail to Harlequin Reader Service®

3010 Walden Avenue
P.O. Box 1867
Buffalo, N.Y. 14240-1867

YES! Please send me 4 free Harlequin Temptation® novels and my free surprise gift. Then send me 4 brand-new novels every month, which I will receive before they appear in bookstores. Bill me at the low price of $2.90 each plus 25¢ delivery and applicable sales tax, if any.* That's the complete price and a savings of over 10% off the cover prices—quite a bargain! I understand that accepting the books and gift places me under no obligation ever to buy any books. I can always return a shipment and cancel at any time. Even if I never buy another book from Harlequin, the 4 free books and the surprise gift are mine to keep forever.

142 BPA A3UP

Name _____ (PLEASE PRINT)

Address _____ Apt. No. _____

City _____ State _____ Zip _____

This offer is limited to one order per household and not valid to present Harlequin Temptation® subscribers. *Terms and prices are subject to change without notice. Sales tax applicable in N.Y.

UTEMP-696

©1990 Harlequin Enterprises Limited

It's hot...and it's out of control!

Beginning this spring, Temptation turns up the *heat*. Look for these bold, provocative, *ultra*sexy books!

#629 OUTRAGEOUS
by Lori Foster (April 1997)

#639 RESTLESS NIGHTS
by Tiffany White (June 1997)

#649 NIGHT RHYTHMS
by Elda Minger (Sept. 1997)

BLAZE: Red-hot reads—only from

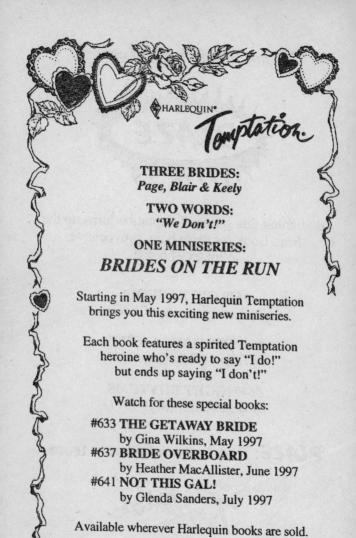

HARLEQUIN®

Temptation

THREE BRIDES:
Page, Blair & Keely

TWO WORDS:
"We Don't!"

ONE MINISERIES:

BRIDES ON THE RUN

Starting in May 1997, Harlequin Temptation
brings you this exciting new miniseries.

Each book features a spirited Temptation
heroine who's ready to say "I do!"
but ends up saying "I don't!"

Watch for these special books:

#633 **THE GETAWAY BRIDE**
by Gina Wilkins, May 1997
#637 **BRIDE OVERBOARD**
by Heather MacAllister, June 1997
#641 **NOT THIS GAL!**
by Glenda Sanders, July 1997

Available wherever Harlequin books are sold.

BRUN-R

And the Winner Is... You!

...when you pick up these great titles from our new promotion at your favorite retail outlet this June!

Diana Palmer
The Case of the Mesmerizing Boss

Betty Neels
The Convenient Wife

Annette Broadrick
Irresistible

Emma Darcy
A Wedding to Remember

Rachel Lee
Lost Warriors

Marie Ferrarella
Father Goose

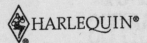 

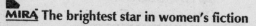

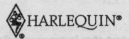

As Seen on TV!

Free Gift Offer

With a Free Gift proof-of-purchase
from any Harlequin® book, you can receive
a beautiful cubic zirconia pendant.

This stunning marquise-shaped stone is a genuine cubic
zirconia—accented by an 18" gold tone necklace.
(Approximate retail value $19.95)

Send for yours today...
compliments of ⟨◇⟩ HARLEQUIN®

To receive your free gift, a cubic zirconia pendant, send us one original proof-of-purchase, photocopies not accepted, from the back of any Harlequin Romance®, Harlequin Presents®, Harlequin Temptation®, Harlequin Superromance®, Harlequin Intrigue®, Harlequin American Romance®, or Harlequin Historicals® title available at your favorite retail outlet, together with the Free Gift Certificate, plus a check or money order for $1.65 U.S./$2.15 CAN. (do not send cash) to cover postage and handling, payable to Harlequin Free Gift Offer. We will send you the specified gift. Allow 6 to 8 weeks for delivery. Offer good until December 31, 1997, or while quantities last. Offer valid in the U.S. and Canada only.

Free Gift Certificate

Name: _____

Address: _____

City: _____ State/Province: _____ Zip/Postal Code: _____

Mail this certificate, one proof-of-purchase and a check or money order for postage and handling to: HARLEQUIN FREE GIFT OFFER 1997. In the U.S.: 3010 Walden Avenue, P.O. Box 9071, Buffalo NY 14269-9057. In Canada: P.O. Box 604, Fort Erie, Ontario L2Z 5X3.

FREE GIFT OFFER   084-KEZ

ONE PROOF-OF-PURCHASE

To collect your fabulous FREE GIFT, a cubic zirconia pendant, you must include this original proof-of-purchase for each gift with the properly completed Free Gift Certificate.

084-KEZR